PLEASURE AND POWER

A NOVEL

Doug Brendel

D1056173

Dragonhead
Press

www.DougBrendel.com

Printed in the United States of America

PLEASURE AND POWER

Prologue

Maddie swings, and the new boy flinches. Ruby's heart skips. It always does.

Maddie is not hefty, which is part of why it's a surprise to the boy. She's long, even for sixteen. You might imagine she's twenty. Her breasts are round but her hips are narrow and her legs are a filly's — stilts. The other girls her age are half a head shorter. Ruby, her younger sister, feels awfully round, awfully short and soft. But her eyes follow Maddie with mostly adoration, hardly any jealousy.

Their mother, Deenah, a huge woman with marvelously delicate fingers, does Maddie's hair in endless narrow braids. They become tight lines of black light when Maddie lets them dangle, and even when she pulls them back, the gleaming streaks make her taller, longer. An educated person might use the word *lithe* — but there are no educated folk here, in the part of Leland they call darktown, where the Negroes live.

Ruby, just fourteen, just pulls her hair back and ties it behind her head. To mimic Maddie would be futile.

The new boy doesn't think Maddie is strong. Her arms are smooth. But when she swings that bat, a fire shoots through her, slicing off of her shoulders and elbows, her wrists and knuckles, so that the new boy has the momentary sensation of a burning saucer flying directly at him. The ragged ball tears past his left ear so fast that it's well past second base before his body can react, and then he ripples — his neck and knees buckling at the same moment, his hips shuddering the opposite way to keep his balance. Ruby's eyes follow Maddie as she flies, her long legs electric. The new boy whirls to peer into the outfield, where boys are flinging themselves toward the escaping ball. Maddie is rounding second base as Ruby turns to look at the new boy. His skin is light enough that he flushes as the infielders giggle.

"Maddie scare ya?" one of them calls.

The new boy bunches up his mouth and exhales through his nose. Maddie leans on a knee at third base, breathing hard, unsmiling. She's played well as long as Ruby can remember. They used sticks for a long time — until finally, a couple years ago, Tobias Farley produced an actual bat. All the neighbor kids crowded around it. It was rough and splintery, but only on the surface: no deep cracks or splits. Tobias claimed a white boy threw it away after getting a new one for Christmas, and why not pull it out of the trash? Ruby didn't believe him but she didn't care. She watched Maddie close her hands around the coarse neck and let the solid weight of the wood pull against her forearms. The other children yammered but Ruby was silent, as Maddie turned away a step or two and brought the bat up over one shoulder. Maddie and Ruby had watched white boys play with a real bat. They sometimes crawled close enough to the white people's park, in under the line of tangled shrubs beyond left field. Maddie squinted at their hands and, back on the dirt field in her own part of town, she mimicked them, teaching herself to slash and sting the ball, even with a stick. But now, thanks to Tobias, *a bat*. Ruby watched her sister lean into it and rotate it around in front of her body. A kind of warmth seemed to flow directly out of her arms into the wood as she moved.

"Try it!" Ruby had cried, her round face radiant. No one else haggled for first try. Everybody knew: If anyone could test a real bat, it would be Maddie.

She stepped to the plate — a mostly flat rock in a scraped-out hollow in the dirt — and Tobias pitched the pitiful, floppy-skinned baseball. Maddie ripped the bat around to meet it. The wood made a sharp cluck as it struck, and the ball's stuffings exploded. Maddie stood wide-eyed, a stunned angel in a halo of twine dust. Ruby and the other children screamed, delighted, and the carcass of the baseball crumpled to the earth, a mess of leather and string clinging to the rubber-coated heart.

By now, Ruby is unsurprised by the surprise. A new child in town is always astonished by Maddie at bat. Ruby almost might have snickered at this newest new boy, a braggart who insisted on pitching because that's what he did back in West Virginia. But she doesn't bother. After Maddie's first at-bat, Ruby always sees the flicker of fear in a new boy's eyes. The pitches arrive nervous after that.

In the distance, a spoon strikes a frying pan four times.

"No, finish!" Ruby calls. But she knows it's pointless. Maddie, a "good child," is already off, her legs gliding across the dusty field toward home. Mama calls, and the game is over for Maddie. Ruby trudges in her sister's wake. The other children grumble. Some half-heartedly ask, "Wanna keep on?" But they know supper is nearly on all over darktown.

Ruby sees the new boy fall into step beside Maddie, looking sideways and up at her. He's shorter, and has to take a fifth step to each of her four, hopping a bit to keep up.

Maddie turns as she moves, smiling the slightest smile. "What's your name?"

"Henry."

"I didn't mean to scare you."

"You didn't scare me!" he squeaks.

Maddie keeps her fluid stride but touches his upper arm. "Sorry anyway."

Henry sighs heavily as he bumps along. To Ruby, Maddie hardly seems to be moving, yet Henry can hardly keep pace. Toward the edge of the vast dirt field, patches of forlorn grass hold their own. The children always call it the dirt field — it's nothing more than an uncertain square of land where there isn't anything, a brown buffer between the black and white parts of Leland, Ohio. To Ruby, growing up here, the dirt field is a sprawling sunbaked paradise of baseball and footraces and big kids' fistfights and imaginary wars and bug-catching. But at the farthest edge of the field lies the reality of a bumpy street, once paved in neat rectangles of brick, now cracked and crumbled, with haggard shoots of the same sad grass. Across the street are the first of the houses of darktown, huddled close and hovering around the south side of the vast dirt field, houses drawn in thin and tilted lines, paint worn away to show the wood or tin or block beneath.

Ruby hurries to catch up, her feet thumping. "Where you live?" she asks.

"Three streets." Henry gestures, falling behind Maddie to walk alongside Ruby. "We had to move. My uncle got in trouble. My cousin Raymond plays real ball."

"Real ball? What was we playin'?"

"He's a grownup. He plays in a league."

"League? What kind of league?"

"Colored. Up by Pittsburgh. He's supposed to come visit us because of my uncle." He looks at Maddie, now far ahead.

"She's my sister," Ruby says.

"My cousin Raymond won't believe her."

"What?" Maddie calls, looking over her shoulder. She sees her sister lagging. "Ruby!"

"When he sees you hit!" Henry calls to her. "I'll bring him to watch you!"

Maddie wrinkles her forehead and smiles at the same time. "Why? No grownup's gonna want to watch a kid play baseball."

Henry peels away, now trotting backwards, on a diagonal toward his own house. Maddie stops short, her long braids dancing, waiting for some kind of answer.

"Because you're amazing!" he cries.

Ruby sees Maddie's face flash warm. For an instant Maddie and the boy are looking at each other. Then Maddie whirls, turning away quickly — but Ruby sees how she has relished the moment. Henry has already turned and dashed away.

"Ruby!" Maddie barks as she turns again to run toward home. "Mama's gonna tan your hide!"

* * *

Henry's grownup cousin Raymond thinks the kid is crazy, but the boy is so jumpy and goofy about it that he agrees to walk over to this "dirt field" and see this girl swing a bat. As they approach, the game stops, and everyone turns to watch. Rarely have any of the children seen an adult on the dirt field. Here, striding steadily toward them, is a behemoth carrying a baseball glove — and a little bug of a boy flitting all around him.

"There she is," Henry announces. "Maddie Tillmore. This is my cousin Raymond." Henry turns to the rest of the group. "He plays in a league up by Pittsburgh."

The children stand in a silent semi-circle of awe.

"How do you do," Maddie offers quietly.

Raymond stands a head taller than she. His arms and neck are stout with muscles. His mouth is crooked with a smirk.

"Henry says you can hit the ball."

"Oh Lord yes!" Henry wheezes.

"Henry, please," Maddie says. She looks at Raymond's eyes and sees them mocking her. "I didn't ask Henry to make you do this."

Raymond puts up his palms. "Right. How about if you hit me a few?"

Tobias Farley, dazed till now, jerks the bat forward for Maddie to take. Ruby is holding the ball. She looks down at it and feels ashamed. Her finger covers the rubber where it's exposed. Ruby can't bring herself to toss the ball, not this ball, not to a man who played in a league. She steps carefully to just an arm's length from him and holds the object out for him to take. He turns the tattered thing over in his fingers and half-grins, shaking his head.

"That is one shitty ball," he chuckles.

He walks to what serves as the pitcher's mound, a rough square dug up by children's toes. The children stand like statues. Raymond looks around.

"Y'all want to field for me?"

Their faces do not change. But they move silently into their places. Maddie stands ready over home plate, and Raymond turns to face her.

"Okay, let's try this."

His arm swings back like a pendulum and rocks forward. The ball swoops in a great arc and over the plate. Maddie doesn't move — Tobias catches the ball — then Maddie straightens up with a puzzled face. The other children begin to titter.

"Uh, we don't play underhand," Maddie says, and the children's giggles sputter alive.

Raymond receives the ball and tips his head a bit.

"Huh. Right."

He takes a breath, winds up, and pitches. The bat flashes. It sounds like a gunshot. The ball shrieks over Raymond's head. He has to plant a foot to get his bearings. Ruby watches Maddie fly to second base, then turns to look at Raymond. He's scowling — a hollow scowl, like the face of a man caught in a lie. He looks back at Maddie, then at Henry, then back at Maddie. His mouth opens on a word, but no word comes out.

Henry wiggles his eyebrows. "See?"

Raymond looks at the dirt and rubs the back of his neck.

"God damn," he says. He bites at the inside of his mouth.

Henry makes a big-eyed face at Maddie. She scratches something itchy on her ear.

"I told you," Henry reminds Raymond.

"Yeah, shut up," Raymond responds, still frowning. "Uh, Maddie."

"Yes sir," she answers.

"Let's try another one, all right?"

"Sure." She's moving smoothly back toward home plate. She picks up the bat and gets ready.

Ruby watches as Raymond looks at the ground and blinks slowly. Finally he blows out a big breath through his mouth and looks at Maddie. He takes a pause, then goes into his windup. The ball rockets out of his hand — Maddie erupts, Ruby's heart thumps — and in a lightning flash, the ball smashes back into Raymond's glove, directly in front of his face, knocking him back a step.

"Oh," Maddie croaks. "That wasn't too good!"

Raymond lowers the glove from his face and looks at the ball that almost beaned him. For a second, his face is a slate of shock, retroactive terror. Then Ruby sees the veins thicken with embarrassment on his temples, even as he shifts his weight. Ruby has seen this from plenty of new kids, trying to look casual.

"Do you want me to hit another one?" Maddie asks softly. "I can do better."

Raymond snorts.

"Let her show ya," Henry calls.

Raymond looks up. His jaw is tight, his eyes a little glassy.

"Sure," he murmurs.

He rubs the back of his neck again. He stands still for only a second. Then he winds up.

In that final second, Ruby can see that his windup isn't right. He's in too much of a hurry. There's a tension in his body, like a spring drawn tight through the middle of him. But the ball is in Maddie's face before she can pull out of the way. It takes only an inkling for her to twitch — just a bit to one side — and the ball crashes into her skull just above her left temple. The force of it punches her backward off her feet; the bat seems to float out of her hands. Her body and the bat crash into the dirt together, puffs of dirt jumping out from under them.

Everyone freezes. Silence.

"Maddie!" Ruby screams. But she's frozen too.

"Jesus, oh Jesus," Raymond groans from deep in his throat. Then he's kneeling over her and the children are all around like stricken flies and Henry is jabbering: "You hit her! You hit her!" Ruby, standing near Maddie's bloody head, her face wrenched, begins to suck air and let out a shrill, almost silent scream, over and over.

"Take her home!" Henry is wailing. "Carry her home!" The children began crying and shouting.

"No! Don't move her!" Raymond yells. "Jesus! Get her mother! Get a doctor!"

Henry stands paralyzed by panic.

"Henry!" Raymond screams. "Damn it!"

Henry points to Ruby. "That's her sister!"

Raymond twists to look up at Ruby. She's lost in her rhythmic panting. He grabs her wrist and yanks hard.

"Go tell your mother. Now!"

Ruby falls silent, looking in horror at him. When she opens her mouth, another sound comes out, hideously — a single-breath scream that slashes everyone else to silence. There's another split-second of stone-cold stillness. Then, finally, she forces herself to hurl about and flee toward home. Some of the children scramble after her. Among those left behind, the chaotic babbling and bawling begin again.

"Is she dead?"

"Maddie's dying!"

"She's dead!"

But Maddie's chest is moving, and her mouth begins to open. "Gah!" Raymond blurts, startled. Her lips come together, then part. Her throat seems to flex. Raymond grits his teeth. "Talk to me," he growls. "Talk to me, Maddie."

"Bee," she whispers, her eyes still closed.

"Yes, Jesus, yes," Raymond pleads.

"Bee," Maddie whispers again. "Bee. Key."

Raymond is drenched in sweat, and now sobs begin to choke him. "What. What. *Maddie!* Talk to me!"

"Bee, key," she mouths.

Raymond's eyes are watery. Maddie's forehead wrinkles.

"Bee, key," she says again.

He looks away. His face twists. "Jesus in heaven help her."

"Bee, key."

An echo of anguish reaches the dirt field. Raymond looks toward the street and sees an enormous woman, her legs pounding up desperate clouds of dust, an almost supernatural cry riding ahead of her through the thick air.

"Eee! Eee!"

Maddie's face clenches.

"Bee, key," she urges.

Raymond leans back, away from Maddie, as Deenah approaches, Ruby following close. The woman closes in with astonishing grace on the fallen girl, folding herself silently over her baby. She lays her hands gently on either side of her daughter's face. The woman's eyes crunch closed.

"Sweet Jesus in heaven," she moans.

Maddie moans in response. The woman looks sharply into her face.

"Bee, key," Maddie whispers.

Her mother's face opens with a start.

"Bee key," Maddie repeats.

"Oh lordy," Deenah gulps.

Raymond shivers. "What," he rasps.

"Bee key."

Deenah's eyes draw closed, and she swallows pain.

"What?" Raymond begs.

"Bee key," Maddie breathes. "Bee key, bee key."

The big woman looks down at her daughter again, then she turns her face away and bawls huge tears. It's the kind of crying that opens the mouth and shows the teeth. She gurgles as she cries.

"Mama?" Ruby whimpers, sounding younger than fourteen.

"She's a baby again," Deenah mourns. "She wants the nipple."

Raymond squints harder, as if this will make sense of it. "What?" he insists.

"Bee key," Maddie laments softly.

"Binky," Deenah replies. "She wants her binky."

1.

The sweet stench of rubber hung in the air six days a week.

On Sunday, the factory was closed, of course, but otherwise the entire complex clanged and whirred and chattered almost around the clock.

Up in Akron, the great rubber companies had risen up like monolithic beasts, sprawling over acres of land and commanding the attention of thousands of workers. They not only fabricated millions of tires but also churned out rivers of rubber — dark rubber, pale rubber, hard, soft — to be heated and shaped and cooled and molded and pressed for a thousand other uses. Along the railroad tracks and major roads that snaked away from Akron in all directions, factories and shops rose up and took form, spawned by the flow of rubber.

By 1940, Chester Arthur Fivecoat was already the wealthiest man in Leland, by virtue of inherited money, but he had an entrepreneurial urge that could not be controlled. Rubber was revenue. Tires didn't interest him, because to buy a tire you needed a car, and to buy a car you needed a major investment, and to make a major investment you needed time.

Centered between his old-fashioned mutton-chop sideburns, Fivecoat's eyes danced with a vision of small things: O-rings inside machines, tubes and hoses for equipment, things that get hot and dry and soon crack and need to be replaced; and household items, things you buy often, things that wear out or get lost or become damaged and must be replaced. Things made with rubber. Not the high-grade rubber that Goodyear insisted on. Fivecoat only needed the cheap rubber.

He built Leland Supply Company, a striking red brick cube, and began producing it all: hot water bottles, stoppers, nipples, balls, gaskets, bellows, pads, bands, seals, liners, grips, plugs, guards to keep blades from cutting when they weren't supposed to — whatever he could find another company to purchase in quantity.

Workers came from all over Leland. Negroes had to come through a considerable stretch of town to get to the job, which inspired some fussing by white residents in the first year or two. But there were no incidents, and by the mid-1940s it was commonplace to see a Negro walking or riding a wobbly bicycle through Leland.

*   *   *

When Jake Valentine left Leland after high school, he didn't intend to return. He said he was heading to college out east, but it didn't work out that way. He saw the sights, worked a bit, met some people, observed the city ways, learned some of them. When the draft started, Jake's lottery number was lucky. When he finally decided to enroll in classes, he was one of the oldest students in the classroom. College, he found, was easy for someone already in his mid-twenties. The prof wanted a composition — "How have party politics shifted since Truman became President?" — but on the day of the deadline, Jake hadn't begun it. Instead, he spoke with the prof privately; the professor soon admitted that the paper wasn't all that important. Jake had something much more interesting in mind: he would stage the concepts, using other students to represent political groups and their leaders. It would only take an additional week to produce. The prof was eager to see such a thing, and happy to wait.

College was easy.

Jake was still a freshman when he met sophomore Tyler Clendennon, who would under no circumstances lend out the black LaSalle his father had sent with him to school. But Jake spoke with him privately, and soon Tyler was eager to lend out the LaSalle, because a blind date could be arranged for him with Julia Haskell. Julia wouldn't give Tyler a thing, but Tyler nonetheless remained in awe of Jake Valentine.

College was fun.

A classmate in Language Arts as it turned out was eager to give up his Saturdays for those two months for Jake's project. Somehow, he did most of the work and still thought the world of Jake. A girl named Liza Grace as it turned out was eager to let Jake open her blouse. Even after it was over, somehow Liza Grace still adored him — or he assumed so; she fluttered her eyelashes involuntarily whenever she saw him on campus.

College was good.

Jake loved the energy of the east, the motion and the noise of the cities. He loved the hustling, he loved the competition. The women were sharp and beautiful. But there were also a million other Jake Valentines there — with equally handsome square jaws, equally blond hair gleaming straight back from their foreheads, equally ready smiles. Jake looked ahead and looked back, and Leland had its own allure. The men of Leland were older, or if they weren't older, they seemed older. Or if they didn't seem older, they seemed simpler.

And now, going up in the lag between his first and last years away, there was Leland Supply. Jake could stand two streets away and still see the fancy blue lettering of the company name at the top of the building's face. In quiet, low-slung Leland, this was big. The east was fine; he could do well in the big city. But here, in Leland, he might do even better. A smaller pond.

In the break between semesters, in the middle of his final year away from Leland, Jake made an appointment to see Mr. Fivecoat and ask him for a job in sales. He was 26 years old, but his only jacket was a tweedy number, barely long enough in the sleeves to conceal the frayed edges of his shirt cuffs.

"Sit."

Fivecoat had a deep brown leather chair for visitors.

"What have you learned in college, Mr. Valentine?"

Jake smiled out of one side of his mouth and crossed his legs. "Nothing, sir."

Fivecoat coughed.

"May I speak frankly, sir?" Jake asked.

"Too late," Fivecoat huffed.

"Nothing in college, at least nothing about selling," Jake continued. "Everything I've learned about selling I've learned outside of class."

Fivecoat's eyes narrowed. "And that might be along what lines?"

"I've learned I can talk people into things."

"Indeed."

Jake leaned forward in the big chair, elbows on his knees and his hands in motion before him.

"You see a need — for hot water bottles or rubber bands or whatever — and you fill the need. That's great. There's an art to seeing the need and meeting it. I admire you for that."

Fivecoat waved a hand. "Yes, right. Please. Skip that."

"But there's more money to be made, sir."

Fivecoat looked at him sharply — and now he leaned forward too.

"If we create the need," Jake said. "If we inspire the need."

Fivecoat cocked his head to one side.

"I invent hunger," Jake said evenly.

"How?" Fivecoat asked.

Jake sat back. "I don't know. People like me, and I talk them into things. And after I talk them into it, they still like me."

Fivecoat stood up. Jake stood up.

"Sit."

Jake's eyebrows went up, and he smiled warmly. "Thank you, sir."

"I'm just straightening my knees," Fivecoat groused. "Can't keep them bent very long anymore."

Jake sat down smoothly and crossed his legs. Fivecoat paced painfully behind his desk, grunting with each left-footed step.

"I've never needed a salesman. I'm my own salesman. Word of mouth is the best salesman I've ever had."

Jake inhaled and waited.

"But everybody's getting into it now. Crayson over in Bellham. That goddam MacIntyre down in Blue Ridge. I tried to buy him out, the son of a bitch wouldn't budge."

Fivecoat put both hands on the back of his chair and leaned hard on it. "I was the first in the county. Now, gotta sell more just to stay even."

"Yes, sir," Jake said quietly.

"My damn knees can't do it."

"I'm sorry, sir."

"Hell you are," Fivecoat rumbled. But then he looked sharply at Jake, and his eyes glinted with a hint of a smile.

"Let's try it. Straight commission."

"Thank you, sir," Jake replied with a nod. "I have one more semester. I'll be available to begin the first Monday in June."

"I'll pay you ten cents for every dollar you bring in," Fivecoat went on. "You'll get a bank draft on the first working day of every month."

Jake almost let the arithmetic take his breath — but he recovered in a flash.

"I'll begin in the morning if you like."

"Yes. Good." He reached into his jacket pocket. "Unless you embarrass me, the risk is all yours," Fivecoat grumped. "So I'm going to risk something myself."

He pulled out a narrow leather book, opened it, and withdrew several green bills.

"Here's sixty dollars, Mr. Valentine," he said, holding the money out. "Get yourself some clothes."

Jake stood and took the paper.

"I'm on my way." And he wheeled for the office door.

* * *

Jake found that DiBanno the tailor was happy to make three new suits for the price of two for someone who would be out and about representing Mr. Fivecoat and Leland Supply. After that, it was easy to sell, for example, rubber bands to Larson Patterson, the owner of the general store in Ulrich Corners, when he had only been buying nipples and hot water bottles before. Jake found that a number of owners of stores and small factories and businesses in nearby towns — Paysville, Yardley, Ulrich Corners, Daunton — were buying some of Leland Supply's products but had no idea many of the factory's other products were even available. Leland Supply had begun manufacturing rubber footings for the legs of stools and cabinets only when the owner of McCarey Industrial inquired. Yet McCarey Industrial — by far Leland's biggest footings customer — had never ordered a single doorstop. Until now.

The woman managing purchases for Gaines Construction over in Sterling decided yes, it would be a nice touch to provide their new construction customers with a doorstop for every door, and she would be happy to buy their doorstops from Jake at Leland Supply. And the manager of Nanceville Household in Nanceville, at first apathetic, let his wife talk him into buying their next supply of bathmats from this earnest young Mr. Valentine. A middle-aged woman, who clearly colored her hair, handled purchasing for Zanesworth's over in Verbena, and they had no real market for hot water bottles. But Jake liked her — she

could sense it, when she looked into his smiling brown eyes —
and before he departed, she had placed an order for twenty.

He was able to trade his wretched Buick for a black LaSalle of
his own, newer than Tyler Clendennon's. He was also able to
move out of the rented room over the print shop on the square
downtown — a room where the smell of ink oozed from the
plaster — and into a small white house rented out by the
Eldridges, who were going to Europe for a year because of Iona
Eldridge's sister's illness.

Here, Jake was at last able to unpack his life. His parents had
been elderly — his mother was thought too sickly to have children
until, late in her life, Jake came along. In his freshman year at
college, his parents had set out by automobile for Monroeville,
Pennsylvania, to visit Jake's uncle, but had died on the way in a
ferocious train wreck. Debts and taxes took the house and the five
acres it sat on just inside the county line. Jake had come home
from school, gathered up as many belongings as he could, stored
half a dozen trunks in the back of Eric Colworth's father's barn,
and returned to college. Now, finally, the trunks came out, the
books and photographs, a phonograph, gardening tools, kitchenware. Jake put them in the various rooms and positions where
they seemed to belong, then washed up and dressed up and got
into the LaSalle and headed north, in the swelter of summer, up
the road to Karney's.

* * *

There was always music and usually dancing. A young woman
with short black hair sat at the bar, smoking a cigarette and idly
watching the dance floor. Jake took the stool next to her.

"Buy you a drink, if you'll let me."

Her face swiveled to meet his. "If that means let you buy me a
drink, okay."

He grinned and wiggled two fingers at Rory behind the bar.

"You do me a grave injustice, young lady," Jake said with a mock frown. "I am a man of honor." He thrust out a hand. "Jake Valentine."

She took it. "Paula Ricard." Her voice was low — not throaty, but smooth.

"Shall I get us a table?"

"I'm comfortable here."

Rory set down a pair of martinis.

"Hm," she murmured. "What makes you think this is what I want?"

Jake leaned an elbow on the bar. "Paula my dear, if you don't want a dry martini, I shall sacrifice by drinking them both. What would you like?"

She took one of the glasses and lifted it, unsmiling. "Peace on earth."

"To peace on earth," Jake answered, clinking her glass. "And it's not even Christmas."

Her dress was sleeveless and silvery, and it glistened as she sipped.

"Care to dance?" Jake asked. "I'm a terrible dancer," he hastened to add with a broad smile, "but I'll be happy to step on you."

Paula looked sideways at him and returned the smile. He had seen that sideways look before. Not from her; he had never met her before. It was the look that came to him when he smiled at a woman, as if his face were assuring her, motioning her in.

"Thanks, no," she replied. "Sorry, man of honor." She stubbed out her cigarette and stirred with the olive, still on the end of the toothpick. "What does a man of honor do, anyway?"

Jake raised his chin playfully. "Haven't you read *Don Quixote*? A man of honor is obligated to gallantly provide for the lady's needs." He lifted his glass. "Or something like that."

Her eyes twinkled. "That's not what I meant. And besides, what if the lady doesn't have any needs?"

"No needs? He is dashed!" Jake cried. She rolled her eyes, then had to suppress a giggle. He liked the effect, and raised his voice even more. "The man of honor is ruined! He is shattered!"

"Shh!" She ducked her head reflexively.

"He is unneeded!" And louder yet, over the music. "He is lost!"

She squealed through her gritted teeth and reached out to squeeze his forearm. "Stop it!" she sputtered, but she was wincing with glee.

Jake stopped suddenly and let his shoulders slump forward.

"Uh!" he groaned quietly. "Thank you so much." He reached over and closed his fingers around her wrist. "Thank you for taking my arm and making me stop."

Paula could not stop grinning. She took another sip.

He wagged his head and arched an eyebrow at her. "And see that it doesn't happen again," he quipped. "Such an embarrassing scene! We have your reputation to uphold."

"My reputation," she echoed. "Jesus." She lit another.

"Imagine what people will think," Jake shot back, "if the man you're with is squalling like a lunatic!"

She nodded big. "Yes! Just imagine!"

Jake glowered and turned stern. "You need reputation management, young lady! You need reputation protection!"

Paula half-shrugged. "That's for sure, isn't it."

Jake picked up his glass triumphantly. "I knew you must have a need in there somewhere," he stated, and drank it down. She chuckled low again. He touched her arm, more softly this time, and did not let go. "Fear not, Paula Ricard. You're safe with me."

"But still no peace on earth," she snickered. But her eyes were dancing.

"Rory?" Jake responded with a formal turn of the head. "We will now celebrate the acquisition of peace on earth. Two more."

* * *

It was deep in the night when she turned out of a heavy sleep, and the movement jostled him gently awake. He adjusted his shoulders against the mattress, and a long, delicious stretch swelled through his body. Paula laid a hand on his belly, where the moon made stripes through the blinds. She could see his strong cheekbones, reflecting bluish, and the hard angle of his jaw, and the tiny, pleasing turn at the corners of his mouth. He watched her eyes moving over his face.

"You never answered me," she said tranquilly.

"How's that."

"What does a man of honor do?"

His mouth pulled up into a relaxed smile, and he reached over to draw a finger lazily across her.

"I've already done it."

She closed her eyes. "Sure, sure." Then she opened them again. "For a living, I mean. What do you do, really?"

He stroked her.

"I sell nipples."

She pulled away and sat up. "Come on. Can't you answer just one question straight?" She reached for a pack of cigarettes on the side table.

Jake sat up too. "I do! That's what I do! I sell rubber products! What's the matter with that?"

Paula grimaced. "Nipples? Really?"

"Nipples for baby bottles. Hot water bottles. Rubber gloves. Tubing. Miles of tubing. Little gaskets and seals and rings and things that you never knew were inside things. Do you know how much rubber there is in a refrigerator? Plenty. What do you need?

I got doorstops. Bathmats." She stared at him. "Who do you think sells all that stuff? Somebody's got to do it. Otherwise your doors wouldn't stay open and you'd keep falling down in your bathtub."

She lit a match and sat still for a while, smoking silently, and he settled back down into the sheets. His eyes drifted shut, and sleep crept over him.

"Will I see you tomorrow night?"

"Mm," Jake answered without opening his eyes. "I'm selling up in Summit tomorrow."

He could not remember more of the conversation, if there was any. In the morning she was gone. On his Summit County circuit was Bailey Warehouse, where a girl named Victoria liked him and would spend her lunch hour with him at her place. In Daunton on Tuesday, he called at Freesinger's Sundries for the first time ever and fell into conversation with Mrs. Freesinger herself, who was surprisingly young and pretty and articulate and who within twenty minutes assured him they would be alone. A few evenings later he went to the Club Carioca over in Morton, where he saw a girl alone at the bar and took the stool next to her.

"Buy you a drink, if you'll let me."

"Sure," she replied with a smile.

He took one of her hands in both of his.

"Thank you," he said, with an impish grin.

She was rattled. "You're holding my hand."

"You said you'd let me," he shrugged.

She looked in his eyes, and something there made her let him.

2.

Only one doctor would treat Negroes in Leland, and he could only bandage Maddie Tillmore's wound and suggest that Deenah "wait and see." Deenah sat by Maddie's bed, rocking and praying and weeping. To get liquids into her, Deenah filled a baby bottle, and Maddie sucked eagerly, like a contented infant, eyes rarely opening. Ruby came to the door and went away, came to the door and went away. It was her room too, but she was afraid of what her sister had become. At fourteen, she felt herself shrinking, like Maddie had shrunk. Or was shrinking. Or might shrink. *Maddie? When will you come back?*

Henry rapped softly at the front door on the second day. Ruby shooed him away.

"My cousin Raymond has to go back," Henry said plaintively.

"Let him go!" Ruby snarled. "Mama says she don't want to see his face again."

The next day Henry came again. Ruby glared at him through the screen door.

"I got a letter for your mama," Henry offered, holding up an envelope. "My cousin Raymond knows she don't want to see him, but this says how sorry he is and how can he help."

Ruby didn't move.

"How, can, he, help," Henry repeated, his eyes watery.

Ruby opened the door, snatched the envelope out of his hand, and let the door slap shut.

"I'll give it to her. Now go away."

Deenah could not make herself look at it.

"I'll read it to you, Mama," Ruby suggested.

"Don't matter," Deenah gurgled, rocking steadily, her eyes fixed on Maddie's dull face. "Throw it away."

In her darkness, Maddie could not feed herself. She could not clean herself. Week by week, Ruby watched the lines deepen in her mother's face. Deenah's had been a smooth, bulbous body, but now the flesh grew leathery and the fatty tissue hung in limp globs from her bones. She was always exhausted but could never get to sleep. She spooned mashed fruit into Maddie's mouth and wiped her face afterward. In the dark of night, Ruby could hear the short, sharp hisses of her mother's helpless sniffling.

The ache in Ruby's heart, like a terrible bruise, finally pushed words out, in the nighttime. She speaks softly to Maddie across the gloom between their beds — about her day, about school. Conquering the arithmetic test. Stuart got a new spinning-top. The awful thing Rosalee said about Goldie, except it was true. Terrence claims he saw Miss DuBois holding hands with Mr. Appleton. The words drifted into the murk, longing for an echo, but the echo never came. Yet every night, in hushed tones, Ruby told the tale of her day anyway, spinning out a lifeline to her sister, for herself.

* * *

As long as Ruby could remember, her mother had cleaned people's houses. She scrubbed floors and toilets and tubs, washed dishes, did laundry. She dusted furniture, polished silver, wiped windows. She would get the girls out the door to school, then tie up a bundle of supplies into her apron and lumber down the road. In some years she had been hired to clean colored people's houses, but usually she headed north to the white sections. She never crossed the dirt field; she did not want to be a dusty mess when she arrived. It was enough to be slick with perspiration. Instead, she walked the long way around.

That was over now. Deenah could not leave Maddie, and she would not let Ruby skip school. A few neighbors brought food to the house, just like people bring food after a funeral. But it was impossible to go on. There was no cushion. No recourse. Rent to pay.

"I can clean," Ruby said. "I ain't afraid."

Deenah lowered herself heavily onto the couch, the stale smell
of old upholstery billowing up around her.

"You ain't gonna be no *domestic*," she said, leaning sourly on
the word. "You belong in school. School's your only way."

Ruby watched her mother's eyes sweep away from her, to the
floor.

Deenah sighed, her hands limp in her lap. "But just for a
while," she said, more quietly. "Just till Maddie gets better. Miz
Harold will let you clean instead of me. And the Cranstons. Just
say your sister's sick, and your mama's taking care of her." Her
words came sluggish, in defeat. "Just for the rent."

The next morning, Ruby tied Deenah's apron around her,
bundled up the usual supplies, and walked toward the Harold
house. Each step was tight with nerves. She knocked softly at the
front door, too softly for anyone to hear. She knocked again, with
greater force, three raps that almost startled her. Mrs. Harold
came to the door, a tall, thin woman with wavy white hair.

"Miz Harold, I'm Ruby Tillmore. My mama's Deenah Tillmore. She can't clean for you but I can."

Mrs. Harold arched. "What happened?"

"My sister's sick. She's taking care of her."

"Well," Mrs. Harold answered slowly, turning her head to one
side.

"I'll work hard," Ruby added quickly. "Just as good as my
mama."

Mrs. Harold said nothing.

"We'll sure appreciate the work, please," Ruby said feebly,
unable to keep looking her in the eye. "I'll do good work for
you."

Mrs. Harold released a breath. "All right, we'll see," she said,
backing out of the doorway. "Come in and we'll see."

By midday, Ruby was aching, her knees stinging, her back muscles throbbing. But afterward, Mrs. Harold inspected her work,

and almost smiled a bit of approval as she handed over the money.

Ruby desperately wanted home. Outside the Harold place, she looked longingly to the right, toward darktown. But she thought of walking through the door, so early in the day, and facing her mother. Maybe Deenah would hug her, maybe even cry a little. Maybe she would stroke her face, touch her hair. Maybe she would sit her down to a bowl of soup. But at the end of the day, the loss would still be hanging in the air. Half a day's pay. Deenah would have made it all. Would have worked the whole day. Ruby turned her face to the left, toward the Cranston place, and made her feet go.

* * *

Jake was still breathing hard as he rolled off of Paula onto his back.

"This is better," she said, snuggling into his neck.

"What's better than what?"

"Better than the bars. Being with you. Alone, I mean."

Jake gave out a heavy, spent breath and pushed his arm under and around her. Her skin was moist, and still warm. She did love to talk, afterward; he had sure noticed that. "What are you talking about?"

Paula wiggled her head against him. "I wandered around a long time. Bar to bar, you know. It's better being with you." Her eyes were only inches from his. Her arm was across his chest, her fingers clasped just below his shoulder.

Their faces were too close for Jake's eyes to focus on her. "Well, I'm glad I was adequate for you this evening."

She slipped her fingers around his arm and almost laughed. "I don't mean just tonight."

Jake knew if he waited, she would finally explain.

"Do you know how many times we've been together?"

Jake lay perfectly still, but he felt something inside tighten. "You count?"

"Ten. Starting three months ago tonight."

"You've counted."

"I didn't intend to. I just happened to."

It was at the base of his throat, where the tightness was.

"It's good, with you," she went on. "With us."

Jake hesitated.

"I'll be back," Paula whispered, and pulled away. She didn't bother to pull anything over her naked body as she circled the bed and headed toward the toilet.

Jake reflexively bent the arm he'd had around her, relaxing the bicep. A scent of sex wafted over the bed and settled around his nostrils. He was limp now, wet and cold. When the toilet flushed, Paula emerged and circled back around the foot of the bed, crawling onto it and dropping her face to kiss his belly with a gross noise. Then she straightened up on her knees.

"This place. God. You're successful, Jake Valentine." She gestured. "Nice radio." She dropped her face back down to his stomach and kissed around his navel. "But you need help."

Jake touched her cheek to make her stop. "Help?"

Paula lifted herself onto her hands and knees and faced him. Her face was open, neutral. "It's not a home, Jake. It could be a home."

Jake frowned a bit. "It's home enough."

Her expression didn't change. "We're good together."

Jake felt a pang in his bladder. Paula turned and let her weight drop her onto her back beside him. "Maybe I'm," she said, then paused. "Ahead of you," she finally said, looking at the ceiling. "I thought you," she began again. "You were ready."

They were silent.

"I'm not pushing you," Paula said evenly, reaching for her cigarettes on the nightstand. "God. Do what you want."

He swung his legs away from her. "I gotta piss."

* * *

Meals shrank, little by little.

"I could go across to the mission," Ruby said as Deenah wrung out a pink blouse. "They give food to folks."

"Oh, Ruby," Deenah answered, shaking her head, not looking up.

"Mama."

"I don't wanna be takin' food from white folk."

"Mama," Ruby repeated. "White folk, it don't matter."

Deenah kept at her task.

"Mama," Ruby said again. "We're hungry."

There was no response.

"Mama, I'm hungry every night."

Deenah's fingers stopped. She looked hard at Ruby.

"You tell them your mama is Deenah Tillmore, the house-cleaning colored woman. Say like that: 'House-cleaning colored woman.'" She looked back down at her work. "Tell them your sister is sick, and can we please have some food."

Ruby turned toward the door

"Don't tell them your sister is crazy," Deenah admonished. "They might not count that for sick. Just say she's sick."

"Yes, Mama."

"Don't tell them she's crazy," Deenah repeated. "White folk take crazy people and lock them up."

Ruby's stomach tightened. She dragged her feet across the dirt field. Her puffy legs felt heavy, like wood — yet it seemed she was across the dirt field and into the white section in only seconds. The center of town seemed to rise up before her: in the middle of the square, a statue of a bearded white man with a long gun, ornate columns standing like idols in front of the bank, a million stair steps leading up to the courthouse. This wasn't the nice section, where she cleaned houses. This was where everyone criss-crossed. White people were scurrying. Each one seemed to inspect Ruby as they crossed her field of vision. Between her lungs and her stomach, something twisted. She tried to keep her feet moving.

In one corner of the square, the shoulder-to-shoulder buildings gave way, and through the space, a full street off the square, sat the mission.

It was a big house, or had been a house, but now the walls seemed to lean in on themselves, wheezing sadly. The paint was peeling off the sign over the front door, so that instead of "GOOD SHEPHERD MISSION" it looked more like "OD SHEPHERD MISS." There were rickety stairs leading up to a narrow landing at the front door; Ruby stepped up gingerly. A rectangle on the door said "Please Come In." Ruby turned the big brass sphere — she had never felt such a heavy doorknob — and when she pulled on the door, she jumped a bit at the angry screech of the hinges.

Inside was a small room, an office, with the rest of the house walled off except for a single door, which stood open on a dim corridor. In the office sat a simple desk with a chair behind it, and a visitor's chair of torn green leather. Ruby hesitated, uneasy about closing the front door behind her. Then she jumped a bit again to hear the sudden konking of sturdy shoes coming down a wooden staircase. Into the doorway stepped a young white woman, maybe in her twenties, in a long navy blue dress, carrying a magazine. She stopped short at the sight of Ruby, whose dark round face was backlighted by the outdoors, her hair pulled back tight.

"Oh my," the white woman said.

"Excuse me, ma'am," Ruby said, her fingers rigid on the doorknob, "if I'm in the wrong place."

"No, no," the woman replied with a quick smile, patting down her hair. It was light brown and wavy, brushed back over her ears. "This is the Good Shepherd Mission. Did you want the mission? Come in."

Ruby carefully pulled the door closed behind her.

"Won't you sit down?" The woman gestured to the chair. Ruby sat on the split green leather. It seemed cold and slippery to her fingers.

"What's your name, dear?" asked the woman, sitting behind the desk.

"Ruby." Her voice was twittery. She cleared her throat. "Ruby Tillmore."

"Ruby, it's good to meet you." She reached her hand across the desk. Ruby took it. She shivered imperceptibly. She had never seen her own hand holding a white hand.

"I'm Alice Bohannon."

Ruby licked her upper lip.

"How old are you, Ruby?"

"Fourteen, almost fifteen."

"I see," Alice said. "We don't often have the privilege of welcoming fourteen-year-old ladies here at the mission."

Ruby looked at her. The woman's face was plain, but she was smiling, and Ruby could not identify it as a false smile.

"How may we help you, Ruby?"

Ruby looked at her hands in her lap. Her throat felt tight. "My mama sent me. She's Deenah Tillmore. She cleans houses for people. She sent me to ask about food. My sister's sick."

"Oh my," Alice said. "What's wrong with her?"

Ruby crooked her thumbs together and flexed them. Her forehead felt warm.

"Well," she mumbled, "she's sick, ma'am."

"It would be all right with me if you called me Alice."

Ruby looked at her uneasily. Alice's eyebrows went up as she smiled.

"I would like it if you called me Alice."

Ruby looked down and said nothing.

"I'm sorry your sister is sick. But I'm sure we can help you."

Ruby looked up at her. "Even if I won't tell you?"

"Tell me what?"

"What my sister's sick with."

"We help people who can't help themselves. It's what Jesus did."

Alice stood and stepped around to lean back on the front of the desk. "Ruby, do you want to tell me what's wrong with your sister?"

"No ma'am."

"Then please don't. If you and your family need help, we'd like to help you."

Ruby sat silent. Alice reached out a hand. Ruby didn't take it.

"Would you like to come with me, and we'll see what we can find?"

Ruby let out a sharp breath, a shot of anxiety, and hopped out of the chair. They went through the door down the corridor, then through another door and into a small warehouse. Ruby halted, stunned. Stale smells of cheap wood and cardboard filled the air. Boxes and crates were stacked to the ceiling, a ramshackle castle of cartons and wooden slats. Two elderly white men and a white woman with her hair in a bun were shuffling about, inventory elves.

"This is where we keep everything we've been able to gather," Alice explained as they strolled. "Food and clothes, things for your bathroom." She turned to Ruby, her navy dress swishing, and took the girl's hands. "Ruby, what do you think would help you and your mama and sister the most?"

"Uh," Ruby said. "Uh?"

Alice chuckled. "Oh, Ruby." *I know you don't want to be here.* "Let's pack a box for your mama."

Alice whirled and scooped up a big empty cardboard cube and began swooping along the walls of boxes, popping out cans and cartons and depositing them in her treasure chest. Ruby followed her in silent awe. When the box got too heavy, Alice found a rolling cart, and they kept on pillaging. Ruby's heart pounded at the carelessness. The bounty. Alice was the food angel — no, the food butterfly, floating and flittering from blossom to blossom, drawing only the best nectar and then dancing away.

"It's too heavy!" Alice exulted, trying to leverage the box off the cart. She finally dropped to the floor beside the cart, laughing at Ruby's goofy, mesmerized face.

"Sit down here with me," Alice said, breathing hard. She tried to push a curlicue of her hair back into place. Ruby sat down next to her. Alice wiped her brow.

"Do you live here?" Ruby asked.

"No, I have an apartment off the square," Alice replied.

"Got children?"

"No. I'm not married."

Ruby's eyes turned up to the box on the cart.

"Oh!" Alice tried to wiggle the heavy cart with her foot. "You can't carry this! May I drive you home and give this to your mama?"

Ruby stiffened. "No."

Alice's face darkened. "Ruby, I'm sorry. I didn't mean to worry you. I only want to get this——"

"No. You might see my sister."

Alice took a breath. "You can't carry it."

"Take some out."

"Oh, no!" Alice wailed. "We had such fun collecting it all!" She was still breathing hard. "Would you rather go home and have your mother come back for the food?"

"My mama can't leave Maddie."

"Maddie is your sister?"

"Yes ma'am."

Alice turned her head at an angle. "You know, I would like it if you called me Alice."

"Yes ma'am, Alice."

Alice paused. "Ruby, I'll help you however you'll let me."

Ruby's stomach gurgled.

"Let me."

Alice touched her arm. Ruby's eyes narrowed to see her flesh silhouetted by the pale fingers.

"This is starting to feel like the fox, the goose, and the corn," Alice said. Ruby looked at her blankly. "Do you know that story?" she asked, her hand still at rest on Ruby's skin.

"No ma'am."

"No Alice."

Ruby just looked at her.

Alice arched an eyebrow. "Come on. *No, Alice.*"

Ruby stifled a smile. "No, Alice."

"Thank you, Ruby. I feel much better." She straightened her skirt on her lap. "Are you ready?"

"Yes," Ruby said. Alice waited. Ruby grinned. "Yes, Alice."

Alice formally cleared her throat. "A farmer had a fox, a goose, and a bag of corn, and he needed to get them all across the river. His boat was only big enough to hold two of them at a time. But depending on which ones he left behind on the shore, he might have a problem."

Ruby's brow furrowed.

"Right?" Alice prompted.

Ruby looked hard at her.

"So what did he do?" Alice asked gently, her eyes coaxing her subject. "What would *you* do?"

Ruby looked down at her feet stretched out in front of her on the floor. Finally she turned her grim face back to Alice. "Are you tricking me?"

"No!" Alice laughed.

Ruby exhaled, but didn't look away. "I'd kill that goose and eat it."

Alice blinked, motionless. Her eyebrows shifted a bit. Then she threw her head back and barked with laughter, the cackles bouncing off the warehouse walls.

"This," Alice cried, "is a very good idea!"

Ruby frowned uneasily, but as Alice kept laughing, Ruby let go of an uneasy smile.

"Wonderful!" Alice declared, collecting her breath. "But I was thinking the *fox* might eat the goose, if we left them together."

Ruby stared at her.

"See? Leave the fox and the corn? Carry the goose over the river?"

Ruby's face was motionless. Alice broke into a huge grin.

"See, I'm the fox, and your mother's the goose. We can't be together — or I might gobble her up."

Ruby covered her mouth. "Oh lordy."

"So we'll divide up this food into some smaller boxes. Each one light enough for you to carry. Put them in my car. You and I drive toward where you live, but not all the way. What street do you live on?"

"Polk. I don't think we should."

"We can stop a whole street away if you want. That's like the farmer crossing the river with the goose."

Ruby was looking hard at her again.

"Then I'll stay in the car, and you can carry one box home, make sure it's all right with your mother, and come back to my car for the next box."

Ruby looked at the box, bulging with cans and jars and little boxes. "I don't think so."

Alice slumped a bit.

"I mean, thank you, Alice. But my mama said."

"What did she say, Ruby?"

Ruby wouldn't answer.

"Well, I'll put some of these things in a smaller box for you, so you can take them home. Then come back later, or tomorrow, and get some more."

Ruby looked at her feet again. "Thank you, Alice."

Alice packed a small box — there would have been four times as much food by the other plan. "I'll be praying for your sister," she said as Ruby left. Ruby lugged the box — big and heavy enough that she had to carry it in her arms like a baby — back across the square and out of the white section, across the dirt field, into darktown, to Polk Street, and home.

Deenah was relieved to see her daughter and the food. Ruby told her all about Alice, and the fox and the goose — and pleaded with her to let her come back in Alice's car with the rest of the food. Deenah's eyes darkened.

"Child, no," Deenah groaned, sitting at the spindly kitchen table.

"Please, Mama," Ruby implored. "She can stop over to Yancey Street. I'll walk the rest of the way."

"Mm," Deenah answered, not looking at her.

"Mama, Alice is nice. She don't want to hurt anybody."

Deenah was silent. Her upper lip glistened.

"She's praying for Maddie."

Deenah's head swung up like a lion's. "What did you tell her!" she roared.

"Nothing!" Ruby squeaked. "I said sick! That's all! She's just a praying lady!"

"Oh, Lord, Lord." Deenah wiped at her face with a cloth. "Lord, Jesus."

"Ma, ma," Maddie sang quietly from the bedroom.

"Mama, let me do it. Please. There's plenty more food. She wants us to have it."

"Ma, ma, ma, ma," Maddie said. "Bee, key."

Deenah's breathing was heavy. "They'll take your sister."

Ruby reached out to close her fingers around her mother's sleeve. "No. Please, Mama."

The big woman put her fingers to her forehead. "Yes, all right, child. Jesus help us."

Ruby bolted for the screen door.

"No," Deenah shot after her. "Not now. Tomorrow. Lord Jesus, Ruby, it's almost dark."

Ruby deflated.

She could hardly get to sleep. The next day she was distracted as she mopped and dusted and wiped. Afterward she hurried home, then raced across the dirt field toward the square and the mission.

But behind the heavy door, a white-haired man was sitting at the desk. He smiled, but when Ruby asked, he told her that Alice wasn't at the mission that day. Could he help her?

Ruby didn't answer. She turned back out, clomped down the steps, and dragged home.

3.

When Jake discovered that purchases made by the county government were controlled from a single room in the courthouse building, he came to the square and nearly danced up the steps. Inside, on the frosted glass of the office door was the word "Purchasing." He rapped his knuckles lightly on the door frame and went in. The crowded room, full of file cabinets and shelves, had the feel of a workshop. Facing the desk was a chair for visitors, covered with a fine sheen of dust. The plate on the desk said "Lucille Waldrup."

"Lucille Waldrup," he said cheerily. He took Lucille Waldrup to be in her mid-fifties, stocky, with a simple silver wedding band. "I'm grateful to find you here."

"Yes?" she answered, looking up with a bit of surprise.

"Please forgive me for barging in." He took her hand. "My name is Valentine, and every time I come through this building I think about stopping in to see you."

His smile was so true, she almost smiled back. "Uh," she began. "Please sit down."

"Oh, I won't take your time." He stood, letting go of her hand but leaning into her a bit. "I'm with Leland Supply, so I always notice the kinds of products we make — like the stops for your doors. This is actually my day off; I don't mean to be selling. I'm just in the courthouse on some personal business. But I always see your name — I always find myself thinking."

He crunched up his face like a little boy dreaming of ice cream.

"'Lucille, Lucille. I wonder how she's doing.'" His face opened up now, toward the imaginary sky, into wide-eyed wonder. "She's got a huge job; she's got the public to look out for. Is she faring well? Is the pressure intense——"

He was glittering. Lucille looked half-alarmed. "Sir," she began.

"—Or does she just have the grace and pluck to handle it all?"

"Sir," she said, blushing.

"Jake," he replied. "Jake Valentine."

"Actually, I have work to do. How can I help you?"

He smiled warmly. "Forgive me, Lucille. I shouldn't be so play-ful. I'll try to be more professional."

"Well," she said, looking at her desk. "I don't mean," she be-gan again, but then stopped.

He looked at her now with a different face. Self-conscious, boyish. "Two minutes, then I'll be gone. I want to make sure the county is getting the best value for its money; so many things are made with rubber nowadays; you could squander a lot of money if you weren't getting good prices; I know you've got a lot of county property to care for, and you want to do the best you can; so I just thought I'd come by and see if I could help you."

"Hm, well," Lucille mumbled. "Mr. Valentine."

"Jake."

"Jake. Thank you for your concern." She touched her collar absently. "Of course you know in county government we do ev-erything on written bids."

"Oh yes!" he replied, his palms up. "I'm not — I don't mean to be inquiring officially." His eyes crinkled cheerfully. "I mean, I would be happy to help if you thought I could save the county some money, but only if you thought so."

Lucille touched her hair. "Certainly I would be happy to have you bid on any of our purchases."

"To save the public some money."

"I am always interested in saving money for the public's sake, of course."

"Well, if I could take the forms with me, maybe I could stay in touch with you?"

Lucille stood and turned away toward a file cabinet. "Of course; let me get them for you."

"That would be good. Thank you."

The paperwork rattled as she sifted through it. Jake silently ran his handkerchief over the seat of the chair.

"This is completely off the subject," he began again as he sat down, "and it may not even be appropriate, but," and he cleared his throat a bit, "that is certainly a nice dress."

Lucille stalled at her task. "Oh, it's just," she murmured, without turning around. "Uh, thank you."

"I just appreciate a person who brings a little refinement to their workplace," Jake said. "I didn't mean to overstep."

She stopped again and turned a bit to him. "No, thank you; you're very kind."

He looked at the floor.

"I'm pleased you came by," she continued, turning back to the file drawer. "I mostly do this by telephone, and the mail."

"Oh, Lucille," he said, a new thought. "I don't know your policies" — he scratched at a place on his chin — "but could I get a frame of reference, maybe? Some of the prices you're paying now? Say, just on doorstops, for example."

In the drawer, she was no longer flipping through files. "Well," she began.

"If it's not confidential," he cut in. "I don't want to break any rules!" he laughed.

"Oh my, no," she smiled. "It seems it all ought to be a matter of public record, but" — now she turned to him, holding back a smile — "I've never really understood why it should be any sort of secret."

She laid a blank bid form on her desk and returned to another file drawer. "Let me just get that for you."

"Well, thank you, that will help me a great deal," Jake said.

"I can't remember anybody ever coming in to ask," Lucille said lightly, without turning around.

"It's their loss, I'd say," Jake replied. "I'll certainly keep everything just between you and me. I don't want you to be overrun with obnoxious salesmen!"

"Oh no," Lucille answered. "I wouldn't worry about that."

"Have you been here longer than I realize?" Jake asked.

"Six years. I came over from Judge Zimmerman's chambers."

She found the file and drew it from the drawer.

Then the door rattled open, and they both turned to see a tall, lanky woman in a business suit, glasses down on her nose, who froze at her forward angle of entry, her hand still on the doorknob.

"Oh! Lucille, I am sorry!" she said through her nose. "I didn't realize you had an appointment."

"No, Betty, it's fine," Lucille stammered, guiding the file folder back into its place in the drawer.

Jake was standing. "I beg your pardon; I'm on my way out."

"No no," the new arrival interjected, "I'll come back. I only needed that New London material. I can get it later."

"I'll — let me get it for you," Lucille said.

Betty was bobbing backwards and closing the door behind her.

Lucille exhaled heavily, still standing at the open file cabinet.

"I'm sorry to make things difficult for you," Jake said warmly.

"Oh no." Lucille's fingers returned to the files.

"I've gummed it up."

"No, heavens," Lucille retorted, taking a breath and gathering herself. She yanked the file back out and rolled the drawer shut. "Betty's a good egg. Don't think a thing about it."

She sat down at the desk and opened the folder. Jake sat too. She turned the first sheet of paper, and her eyes ratcheted down the page.

"Here we are," she said. "Stroop Company, in Cleveland." She read the price.

"Oh Lord," Jake warbled. "Lucille, please. Let me help here. The county shouldn't be paying that. The nerve — well — I'm glad I stopped by."

"I am too," she said.

"You should have someone do right by you," he said as he stood, his eyes shining.

"I'll hear from you soon, then, Mr. Valentine?" she asked. "Jake?"

He took her hand, as if to shake it, but he only closed his fingers around it. "Yes." He let go of her hand, picked up the bid form, turned and opened the door. In the doorway he turned back and looked at her, seeming to enjoy her, for a fleeting second. "Thank you so much for this," he said smoothly. Then he was gone.

Betty stepped slowly into the doorway, but she was looking after Jake. Then she turned to look at Lucille, whose face was warm. Betty's eyebrows bent quizzically.

"Who was that?" she asked, nasally.

Lucille sighed. "Some seller."

* * *

Outside, early October had turned warm and sunny. Jake dashed down the courthouse steps, folding the form into his jacket pocket, and broadsided a young woman walking by. She peeped in surprise as she staggered sideways to keep her balance, and her bundle exploded to the ground. Jake snapped to attention, astonished by the collision, then instinctively shot out a hand to her arm, even though she had already recovered. She was not angry; she was smiling a wry smile, one hand touching her wavy brown hair.

"God! Forgive me!"

The woman smiled even more. "A man of prayer," she noted.

Jake blushed. "Not exactly," he said, crouching to gather up her goods. The coarse brown wrapper lay mangled on the sidewalk, and maroon rectangles were clumped and scattered in a rough oval. The woman knelt to help.

"I am so sorry." He looked at what was in his hand. "Are these Bibles?"

"Just New Testaments. We can't afford whole Bibles."

"Oh my God," Jake said, collecting the last of them. "I've struck down a religious woman."

She stood herself straight. "I think religion — and the woman — will survive the blow."

He was trying to stack the little leather-bound books in his arms and get the paper wrapper back around them.

"Here," she said, taking the books and leaving him the paper. "Hold that open."

He did as he was told, with the brown paper open in his hands, as she stacked the New Testaments in neat rows. The original folds in the paper seemed to magically re-appear exactly at the edges of the books.

"Easily done," she said cheerily. She drew up the edges of the paper and folded them over the contents.

"You're a saint for not hating me," Jake said. "I wasn't watching."

"Ha," she replied flatly, taking the bundle out of his hands. "We were both racing." She could tuck the bundle under one arm again now.

"Jake Valentine," he said, hand extended.

"Alice Bohannon." They shook hands. "Jake? Jacob?"

"Yes, actually. Nobody calls me that."

"Jacob," she repeated. "The deceiver."

In her twenties. Hair light brown; a little too mousy, he thought. But she had waved it so nicely.

"Hm?"

"Jacob means deceiver. Schemer. In the Bible, I mean."

Jake's mouth opened a bit, but no words came out.

"It's mysterious," she went on. "I meant no offense." She shrugged, like a schoolgirl. "I like it."

"Pleased to meet you, Alice," Jake said, sheepishly. "Pardon the circumstances."

"Full pardon is granted," she replied pleasantly. "If you'll excuse me?"

Her eyes were greenish. Maybe call them hazel, Jake thought. "Oh. Uh, yes."

She was walking away.

"Miss — Bohannon?"

She stopped and turned. Her face was a simple triangle. She could have had more of a chin. His mind was clicking, but no words registered.

"I — Sorry. Thanks."

"You're welcome, Mr. Valentine. But with a full pardon, no apologies are required."

Her skin seemed a little pale, he thought. She was slender, and her dress was long and narrow on her. Jake watched her go. Her shoes were sensible, but he was surprised by how fluid her motion was. A religious woman would clunk more, he thought.

He had parked his LaSalle a block away; now he wondered exactly where. He looked across the square. Carrasco was fixing the peppermint pole outside his barber shop. Jake rubbed his cheek with the flat of his hand. He could feel the tiniest prickles of his whiskers. He was so blond, he knew they didn't show yet. He looked across the square in the other direction. Alice was still gliding away.

Jake leaned forward and began to trot on a diagonal across the square. He did not want to run. Or at least, be seen running. As he got close, he slowed to keep his shoes quiet on the brick street.

She turned and saw him coming. Her face tilted a bit and she stood still.

"Are you all right?" she asked, her face a blank.

Jake broke stride and settled into a walk. He tried to roll the word nonchalantly. "Sure." He wasn't sure it came out right. It seemed to be taking too long to reach her. "I just — I owe you. I, uh." He was breathing hard. "I try to be a man of honor."

The thin arcs of her eyebrows went up gently, to go with her delicate smile. "You don't understand the idea of full pardon, do you?"

Jake put a hand in his pocket. He took a deep breath. He was off his usual rhythm. "I think even a rotten criminal should feel grateful for it," he finally replied. He pulled his hand back out of his pocket and motioned toward Partridge's. "Buy you a cup of coffee, if you'll let me."

"Hm," Alice responded. "Cherry Coke?"

He tossed his head, recovering. "Let the restitution begin!"

Which she found amusing. And they crossed the square and took a booth in the window and talked till their stomachs grumbled, at which point Jake ordered burgers and refills on the drinks and they continued talking.

It was her day off, but she was working. She was employed by the Good Shepherd Mission, started decades ago by a church three counties over because at the time they had a wealthy parishioner who — too complicated to explain.

"Mostly it's volunteers," she said. "Officially, I keep the accounts and run the office, but there's nobody else, really, so, well, I'm the 'director.'"

"What happens there? At a mission?"

"We give people food, clothing, soap, whatever they need."

"And Bibles."

"Well, there's not much demand for Bibles."

"You've got a few there," Jake said, gesturing to the parcel.

"Yes, they were donated. Churches love to donate Bibles. If I could trade Bibles for food, nobody in Leland would ever go hungry again."

Jake watched her fingers, long and slender, stirring her cherry Coke with the straw. Her nails were neat but short. A working girl's nails.

"This can't be interesting to you."

"It is!" Jake chirped, and then blushed a bit to hear how chirpy he had sounded. "Where do you get the food, and, uh things?"

"From all over — churches, and ladies' groups, and friends of friends — like these New Testaments. A friend of a friend runs a printing plant in Indiana, and they printed too many, so they say, 'Oh! Let's send them to Good Shepherd!'"

"And I clobber you and knock them all over."

"At least it wasn't oatmeal," Alice answered.

"People send you oatmeal?"

"No, it's a joke. Groceries and restaurants give us whatever they can spare — and that's good. We can visit them on a regular schedule."

He found himself looking at the hollow at the base of her neck. Then he caught himself and looked into her eyes again.

"But most donations don't come in on a steady schedule, and volunteers have to be managed, and — well, the real point is to help people, but it takes a lot of time arranging everything so we can be ready for those few minutes when somebody shows up and needs something."

"Anybody can just show up? Anytime?"

"I try to keep the mission open as much as possible. But a lot of people are too embarrassed to visit the mission, so I stay in touch with churches, to find out who might need help. And the police, actually."

"The cops?"

"They tend to know when somebody's in trouble."

Jake didn't realize he was frowning.

"You're frowning."

He started a little, looking up. "Sorry. I just never — thought of it."

She looked at him quizzically.

"People being in trouble, that way," he said.

Alice smiled. "You figure, well, this is 1948, times are good?"

Jake began to speak but then closed his mouth again. Alice laughed. Jake blushed and shifted on the bench.

"I wish more folks from darktown would come in." Alice stirred her cherry Coke again. "I think they think it's a white mission."

"Well, it's white on the outside," Jake said.

"Barely. It needs paint. But of course, paint costs money."

Jake could hardly picture it. Growing up in Leland, he had scarcely registered its presence. It was there but not there. The house had been donated a generation ago — part of the estate of a wealthy religious man from over in Crawford County — but now, if locals noticed it at all, they were generally nervous about it, and tried to look the other way as they walked by. Back in the day, needy men coming for help were supervised by a chaplain and two male assistants, and discreetly kept in the back part of the old house, where they could shower and shave, change into new used clothes, and if necessary spend the night. It was a big house, but not big enough to maintain separate quarters for women, so women could not shower or spend the night. In the early days, there was a chapel service every morning.

"But then came the war," Alice said, "and the chaplain was old, with nobody to replace him, and money was tight, and one problem led to another, I guess. So now, it's just—" She pinched a bit of fallen lettuce from her plate into her mouth. "You do what you can."

Jake kept expecting a false note, the self-righteous tremolo of religiosity, but Alice talked about her work as if she were an auto mechanic. He would not have been surprised if she had prodded him about his own utter heathenism, but she did not go to the subject.

She had come from Trillip, a town so small that even Jake had never heard of it. To Alice, Leland was the big city. Her father was notorious, a nasty drinker of whisky, but he had been slick in his day. "I probably have brothers and sisters — half-brothers and half-sisters — all over northern Ohio," Alice smirked. Her mother, too religious to divorce him, suffered mostly in silence, and finally succumbed when influenza ravaged the area. Alice, a teenager, went to be reared by a great-aunt who was faithful to Christ the King Free Church in Stony Township. Yes, Jake did know Stony Township; he had a tubing account there.

Alice read everything; but college was out of the question. When high school ended, she moved up to Leland. Once a year, Christ the King organized a charity drive to send non-perishables over to Good Shepherd Mission. So Alice knew of the work, and when she visited, the director, old Mr. Johanson, had just lost his office manager to her husband's new job in Toledo. He had been thinking of shutting the place down. A year later, illness prompted old Johanson to retire. Alice was left.

It was not a spectacular face, but her lips — sure, they were somewhat thin, but they were pretty when she talked. Jake was sure she was wearing not a bit of makeup, but her eyes were naturally alive. He enjoyed the way she wrinkled her nose to signal something small or embarrassing — like when she said "Trillip" — like a little girl, but unpretentiously. Her long, narrow hands and fingers moved with a kind of easy elegance. A tiny gold chain around her neck; no rings.

"So that's what I do," Alice said with a bit of a shrug.

Jake did not realize he was resting his face in his hands like a schoolboy until he began to speak and found that his jaw wouldn't move. He blushed and straightened up and tried again.

"Will you always?" he asked.

"What?"

"The mission. You could — I don't know — do something else."

Her eyes were light and bright. "Will you always sell bathmats and doorstops?" she asked without a hint of defensiveness. "You could do something else."

Jake leaned back and let his eyes wander around the café. "In Leland, it's good money."

"Don't you think it helps people?" she asked.

"The mission? Sure."

"No, to sell them bathmats and doorstops."

He looked at her to see if she was teasing him. She was not.

"They're useful." She leaned across the table and grabbed her glass. "What if people had no doorstops! Their doors would flap. It could be dangerous!" There was laughter in her voice, but she wasn't laughing.

Jake ran his hand through his hair. He had almost said "You sound like me" when he realized how lost he was. He did not want her to know he knew how he sounded. His throat felt a little dry, but his glass was empty again. He needed to get his rhythm back. He looked in vain for the waitress.

"I'm not making fun of you," Alice said sweetly. "You help people in your way. I help people in my way." She shrugged her little shrug. "I enjoy helping people. That's all."

"Yes, I guess. I never thought of it like that." He cleared his throat. "Your work seems — mine is——"

He could not find the end of a sentence. Alice was tickled.

"It's a good thing," she said, bailing him out, "that some people only need a doorstop. Not everybody has the kind of trouble that brings them to the mission; thank God for that."

Jake's mind was grasping. Everything he thought to say seemed unseemly. He finally put one arm up over the back of the booth bench and made an attempt.

"Do you find that men are always telling you how beautiful your eyes are?"

But he bit his lip, and wished he hadn't said it.

Alice sat back amiably with her arms at her sides. "Do you find that women are always falling into your arms when you ask them that?"

Jake opened his mouth to speak, but no words came out.

"Jake Valentine," Alice announced, "this has been a lovely day. I will enjoy it over and over again, every time I remember it."

He tried to speak again, but she shook her head ever so slightly.

"Time to go."

In front of Partridge's, he gestured in the direction of the mission. "I could walk you there."

"Thanks, there's no need," she replied, her face still cheerful. "Man of honor! Oh, boy," she chuckled. "Thank you again, Jake. I enjoyed it."

She turned and walked, the brown parcel of New Testaments under one arm.

The words gurgled up out of his throat. "Could I — Could—"

She turned full around, without missing a step, and drawing the parcel up into her crossed arms, she continued sauntering backwards. She was smiling a radiant smile.

"Thank you! It was delightful!"

She spun gracefully around and sailed on.

2

2 of honor?"

She spun again and kept walking backwards. He loved how she did it. Her face was as open and fresh as before. She was far now, and had to raise her voice.

"Honorable behavior!" she called to him. To Jake it seemed she was almost gleeful in proclaiming it.

* * *

The next day, he called on Alice Bohannon at the Good Shepherd Mission, having failed to acquire her home address, let alone permission to call on her there. A roundish Negro girl, hair pulled close to her scalp, was carrying a heavy box out as he arrived. He held the door for her.

"Thank you," Ruby said bashfully, not quite looking him in the eye.

"You gonna be okay with that?" Jake asked as she went by. "It looks awfully heavy."

"I'll be all right, thank you," Ruby replied, clonking carefully down each step.

He watched her as she headed away. Then he turned to go inside.

"Well!" Alice said, bright-eyed. "How can the mission help *you*, young man?"

Jake did better this time; he was on his game, charming and clever — even though to be with her again excited him in a way he could not understand, and when he was alone again afterward, he had to go to the bathroom.

She had a telephone at home; she agreed that he could call her, and he did. But better than that, they went to the Old Bijou to see movies and three times to Chez Chat, the fancy restaurant

up in Sagerstown with a neon cat in a top hat on the roof. They
had lunches back at Partridge's sometimes; sometimes he could
persuade her to let him drive her to Ramsey's, which took twenty
minutes and cut a chunk out of the middle of her day. He did not
suggest going to Karney's, or to the Club Carioca over in Morton.
But Alice was not averse to taking a drink of wine, so they were
able to enjoy Tito's.

His great victory — the achievement that made his spirit crow
— was reserving a Saturday morning and taking her to a strand of
meadow along the Ossowaga and spreading out a blanket and a
picnic meal and then (this was the part he loved best, because she
loved it best) reading poems to her. Even as he read the lines, he
could not believe he was doing it, but her eyes glistened with such
satisfaction that he carried on, never faltering.

He kissed her that day. He was careful not to do it until they
were back in town, but before they got out of the car in front of
her apartment he leaned over and touched his lips to hers. He
intended to be brief, and he was, and he sat back, but something
made him pause before getting out of the car, and then she
leaned over with a hand on his face and kissed him warmly and
deeply.

* * *

I do want it to be true, she told herself, alone that night.
I do love a happy ending.
I do believe in miracles.
She poured herself a glass of milk and sat at her kitchen table.
The kitchen of her childhood, in Trillip, spun around her. She
put her head in her hand and closed her eyes. She could smell the
whisky as her father rumbled from his favorite chair in the next
room.

"Come here, sweetie, gimme a little kiss."

God, I can't fall in love with a boy like him.

"Come on, wifey. Gimme a kiss or I'll beat your ass." Then, a raspy cackle of laughter.

God, please, no.

"Come on, don't you want a little kiss from your old man? Patty Connor likes to gimme a little kiss. Want me to go over to Patty's place and get a kiss?" More cackling.

God, please don't let me become my mother.

"Goddammit, Martha, come here! I oughta walk outa here and never come back."

Tears stung her.

"I've had plenty of women. I don't need this aggravation."

She was breathing hard.

"I'll find me a good woman, goddammit."

Jake can't be like that. He's nice. He would be true.

"Alice, where's my pipe?"

She could hear herself wheezing, and her cheeks were hot, and then cold where the tears left tracks.

"Bring me my pipe, dammit, or I'll break your head."

She clenched her teeth.

"Stop," she said aloud. "Stop it."

Her childhood kitchen began to evaporate. She opened her eyes, lifted the glass to her lips, and finished the milk.

Let me be, Daddy.

* * *

It was a lovely, mild winter. She watched Jake skating into her heart and couldn't stop him. So glib, but so devoted. She held back what she could, but it was less and less. Until there was nothing left to hold. She loved how he loved her.

As she pressed the pencil to the paper, she clenched her teeth, then realized it and forced herself to relax her jaw. She let out a deep breath and began writing.

"Dear Daddy," she began. "I am getting married, and I want you to be there."

Aunt Goldie, her father's mother's sister, asked about his plans.

"Goddammit, I ain't going to no wedding," he grunted.

4.

Ruby smiled broadly as she came through the door.

"Ruby! How are you?"

"I'm good," Ruby answered, beaming.

Alice put down her book and headed for the warehouse door. "Let's see what we can find for you today."

Ruby followed. After six months, she knew the routine. She loved the routine.

"I have good news," Alice said as she plucked an empty box from the stack and moved toward the shelves. "I'm going to be married."

Ruby stopped, eyes wide. "Married," she repeated softly.

"Yes!" Alice reached for a can, put it in the box, then turned to look. Ruby was staring. "Ruby, are you all right?"

Ruby didn't move. "Will you——" Her mouth closed tight.

"What, Ruby? What is it?"

"Will you go away?"

"No! I'll be right here."

Ruby was still.

"He has a house here in town. I'll move in with him." Alice reached out to take Ruby's shoulder in her hand. "I'll still be here at the mission." She squeezed a bit. "It will be fine."

Ruby looked away, at nothing. Alice left her hand there. "Ruby, I'll be here for you."

Ruby's eyes glassed over, reddish.

"I think," she said, then stopped. Then she started again. "I think I want to tell you about my sister." She breathed deeply and looked into Alice's face.

Alice glanced around. "Let's sit down here," she said. "On the floor. Just like the first day we met."

Ruby didn't answer. She simply slumped to the floor. Alice sat down next to her, and waited.

"We was playing baseball, with a man," Ruby began quietly. "Man threw a baseball, hit Maddie in the head."

The air was still. Ruby opened her mouth, but only a sob came out. She covered her eyes.

Alice touched her shoulder again.

Ruby swallowed hard, fists in her eyes. "She's crazy now. Like a baby crazy. Can't talk nothin' but baby talk."

She wheezed with the anguish.

"Mama's takin' care of her."

"Ruby, I'm so sorry," Alice said, fighting back her own tears.

"That man," Ruby gasped. "It's like he killed her, but she's not dead."

Alice's tears spilled onto her face.

"I hate that man," Ruby gurgled. "I hate him."

Alice leaned over to enfold her. It was an awkward hug, the two of them sitting on the floor.

"I hate that man," Ruby said. "I want to kill him." And her body throbbed in Alice's arms.

Alice tried to breathe.

"Oh my dear friend," she finally said, and the sobs finally poured out of her, too. The two could only convulse together, wrapped up like one person, their hearts pounding against each other, and for each other.

When they finally couldn't cry anymore, Alice let her go. They straightened up. Ruby pulled a sleeve across her nose.

"I don't know how to make it better," Alice said, sniffling. "But I want your heart to make it through."

Ruby's face was buried deep in her blouse.

"If you can find a way to forgive that man, whoever he is," Alice said.

Ruby flung herself back, away from her. She couldn't look at her. They stayed still for a long while.

"Jesus taught us," Alice said.

She felt Ruby tensing.

"I'm only saying," Alice continued, breathing heavily, "I don't want you to hurt yourself."

Ruby turned to face her. Ruby's face was a gash, a torn place. But she blinked, and gave Alice an opening.

"People do bad things," Alice said. "Terrible things. But don't let that be you."

Ruby took in a deep breath. A shudder she couldn't stop.

"Ruby, don't let the bad become *you*."

Ruby looked at the floor. She tried to smile. "Is he nice?"

Alice looked puzzled.

"Your man."

"Jake. Yes," Alice answered, with a wide smile. She picked herself up from the floor, and Ruby followed. "He's very nice." She turned back and loaded a couple more cans into the box.

"Have you known him long?" Ruby asked.

"Well," Alice replied, "let's see." She stopped to ponder. "I think about as long as I've known you." Alice grinned at her. "Do you think it's long enough?"

Ruby's eyes moved up and past Alice's face. Alice pivoted to see what she was looking at. Ruby pointed to a jar of something red.

"Could I have some of that?"

Alice reached for it. "Yes! Cherry! Very good."

* * *

She lay on her back in her bed. Her final night alone. Her eyes were unfocused in the dark. She floated back to Trillip. To the house trailer cut open on one end, attached to a wooden shack, a Frankenstein dwelling she never wanted her schoolmates to see. Alice is eight. Her parents' voices are cutting, hardly muffled at all, through the thin walls from their room.

"Stop it."

"Come on."

"Stop it, I said."

"Goddammit, come on."

Did her mother let go a soft laugh? Or was it a choke?

Her mother's voice again, low. "Oh." Then a thin sound, a reedy breath. Alice strained to hear, to somehow see the sound in the darkness. A stifled moan?

Grunting. The achy whine of the springs. A muted cry. Another "Oh." Then silence.

Floating again. Another night. Alice is twelve. Closed up in her room. Her parents are still up.

"The hell I did."

"I'm not a fool, Harv."

"You're with me. What's that make ya?"

"You're so drunk you don't know what you're saying."

Glass clinks unevenly. "I know," then a pause, "I know what I like."

"Christine Riggs. She's a whore."

"So what. Leave me alone."

"You were with Christine Riggs, then you come home to me?"

"I come home," then a pause, "to be a nice guy. Be the husband." He gurgles a bit. "And the father."

"You're pitiful."

Glass clinks again. "Alice needs a nice father. I'm nice."

A chair scrapes against the floor.

"Harvey, you listen to me."

"Ow, let go my arm."

"You listen to me, Harvey Bohannon." Her voice is low and tight, almost a buzz. "You ever touch Alice — you ever lay one finger on that girl — I will kill you."

He snorts.

"I will personally kill you dead."

"Hell, Martha, I ain't doin' nothin' t'Alice. Let go."

"See that you don't, Harv. I'm serious."

"That's sick talk. Crazy sick. Let go, goddammit."

The chair scrapes again.

"You 'bout broke my arm."

"Good."

Alice floats again, forward in time. She's fourteen. Sitting on the floor, reading. Her mother is in the rocker, knitting under lamplight. Her father is out.

"Mommy, you feel right?"

The rocker keeps time, a quiet beep of a squeak at the back end of each arc. "Sure."

"You look gray."

"Just tired, I suppose."

Alice looks back down at her book, but can't read. She looks up again. Her mother's pleasant face, a bit jowly before its time, is tilted down toward her work.

"I heard last night."

Martha's needles keep flashing.

"I know Daddy's mean to you." The words are steady and smooth. No rancor. Just an offering of truth.

Martha rocks and knits in the same silent rhythm.

Alice looks at her book again. "I'm afraid," she says softly.

The rocking chair falls silent. Martha draws a long breath. Then her voice is even, like a ribbon pulled tight. "Your father will not hurt you."

"I don't mean Daddy." Alice looks up. "I'm afraid to get married."

Martha stares at her. There's no movement in her face, but her eyes seem to drift, somehow, into Alice and all the way through her. Martha finally lays the needlework in her lap and sets her lips together.

Alice sits perfectly still. She can smell the yarn in the basket next to the rocker. "He hurts you, doesn't he?"

Martha's head tilts a little to one side.

"In bed. It hurts, doesn't it." Then Alice bites her lip.

Martha's eyes open wide, and her face relaxes, turning a bit sideways. Her cheeks come up into a sheepish smile. "Oh my Lord." Now she lets go of a quick cackle. "Oh, my girl."

Alice's face burns, but she doesn't look away. Her mother's eyes glisten, but not with tears. Alice makes a puzzled face. She was ready for tears.

"You're too young for this, but I will tell you the truth," Martha says, her words rolling a little, like a storyteller's beginning. "There's a lot of bad in life, dear daughter. There's a lot of bad in your daddy. But I don't believe in making more bad than's already bad."

She's looking deep into Alice's eyes. "Some folks think it's bad, what men and women do in bed. Husbands and wives. But I never found it to be bad. I believe God made it for pleasure. So I take the pleasure."

They look at each other awhile, each waiting for the other to speak.

"There's plenty of pain in life," Martha finally says. "But between a wife and a husband, that doesn't have to be more pain. That can be good."

"Sometimes," Alice says, haltingly, "it sounds bad."

Martha laughs. "Well, I don't think I can explain that. I think that's something you'll just have to experience." Her eyes crinkle into a smile, then her face relaxes. "When you're a wife. Then you'll know. You just take the pleasure. Don't let anybody make you any different."

Her eyes drop to her hands, and she begins to work the needles again. Then she stops again.

"You're fourteen. You wait awhile to find a husband. Then you find a good one, and enjoy him." She sighs deeply and lets it out. "A good man will be easier to enjoy."

Alice looks back down at her book, the rocker returns to its rhythmic beeping, and she's floating past the next few days. Her mother grows grayer, something is wrong, the influenza sweeps through Ohio, she's too weak, she slips away. Alice floats past the aching hole in the ground, the aching hole in her heart, the stench of whisky-breath in the kitchen, her father bent over like a vulture at the table, soaked in liquor and rage. The scraping from deep in the well of his throat: "Do whatever the hell you want." His eyes yellow with shame. The tangle of grief and relief as she moves to Great-Aunt Goldie's. The strange weightlessness of high school, as the girl with no parents. Alice floats through graduation. Floats to Leland. To now. To this last night before Jake.

She glides the palm of her hand over her breasts, slowly over her belly, more slowly still inside her thighs. A half-moan escapes. She rolls on her side. She needs to sleep, but her eyes won't close.

* * *

They were married in the tidy little chapel in a corner of the mission. Her great-aunt Goldie came in from Trillip for the wedding. Alice hugged her and kissed her on the cheek.

"Is he coming?"

"No, child, I'm sorry."

Alice exhaled. "I'm not."

Old Mr. Johanson looked terrible. He was shaky on his cane, but strong enough to give the bride away. For best man, Jake turned to his friend Eric Colworth, who had stored Jake's stuff in his father's barn. Leland's justice of the peace officiated.

The newlyweds left Alice's ordinary Ford behind and drove the LaSalle to Erie for a honeymoon, where they stayed in a hotel right on the waterfront. Jake was prepared for Alice to be demure in bed, but she was generous and spontaneous, and her long, lean body responded to him electrically. In daylight, she never looked at him with shame, only with pleasure. Alice moved her things from the apartment off the square into Jake's small white house, and the lifeless orderliness of Jake's belongings was transformed into the ramshackle warmth of a home.

"We have two cars!" Jake yelped. "We're rich folk!"

Alice wrinkled her nose at him.

That Jake was married did not change much of anything for Lucille Waldrup, who was still warmed by his visits. (She loved how he always took her hand when he talked to her.) It did not change anything for Cora Jessup at Randover Appliance, whose husband Gordon was on the town council. ("Oh, Jake, you should be a politician!") Or for Virginia Demitrius who handled purchasing for Ephraim. A visit from Jake Valentine shot the day through with something strong and heady. If he was married, it was all the more delicious that he waggled and teased them as he did. Chester Arthur Fivecoat almost purred as he signed the bank drafts for Jake Valentine.

He was on his way in to Sondwerth's. It was a routine call.

"My my my ..."

The voice was familiar. Jake turned around. "The nipple man."

Paula Ricard was heading into Sondwerth's too.

* * *

Deenah slumped, weary, at the table. Ruby unloaded the box.

"Look, Mama!" she exulted, holding out the jar. "Cherry!"

"Oh, darlin'. That's nice."

Ruby spread out the goods. "I'll put everything away. You rest."

Deenah's eyes drifted across the boxes, the cans, the jars. "Yes."

Ruby opened the cupboard door.

"I don't like this, child."

"It's all right, Mama. It's good. Alice likes it."

Deenah's head turned side to side. "Can't keep doin' this."

"She says that's what the mission is for," Ruby said, moving boxes into their places.

Deenah's face was ashen.

"Can't keep doin' this."

5.

Jake did feel badly about it. He did. It was really just a freak coincidence. He was there, she was there. He had not been prepared to deal with it properly.

He was within two streets of home when a speck of something irritated his eye, and as he pulled at his eyelash, a whiff of sweetness reached his nose. He sniffed at his cuff. Now he couldn't be sure. Was it the scent of Paula Ricard, or just his imagination?

His heart thumped hard. He cursed under his breath and steered the LaSalle to the curb. *Stupid!* he told himself. She had just made herself so — available.

"Jesus," he spat, killing the engine.

He got out, hustled to the front of the car, and opened the hood. He ran his hand along the inside. It was grimy. He closed the hood and rubbed his palms together. He looked at them; they were too dirty. But the smell was right. He fished a handkerchief out of his pocket and ruined it by wiping off most of the grime. Then he turned it over and used the clean side to dab his brow.

Back in the car, he craned his neck to get his face into the rear-view mirror. He watched as he drew two fingers across the side of his neck. It wasn't quite enough. He used four fingers this time. That looked better.

He checked his wrists with his nose. To be sure, he rubbed each palm on the opposite wrist and inhaled again at close range. Adequate. *Stupid fool!*

The handkerchief was a lost cause, too smeared with greasy dirt. He drove around the corner, into an alley, and stopped at a trash can.

* * *

"Don't touch me; I'm a mess!" he crowed as he came through the door.

"What happened?" Alice called, tossing a magazine on the table and coming out of the kitchen.

"I don't know," he sang on his way to the bathroom. "They could put a gun to my head and make me fix a car, and I'd have to let them shoot."

He was running water in the sink as she came into the doorway. "Oh, my!" Her face was its usual radiance. "Here, let me get your cuffs out of the way."

"It may be too late already," Jake said as she turned his cuffs back. "I tried to stay clean."

"Tell me the car didn't break down."

"No, just made some kind of noise," he replied, washing his hands. "I jiggled the hoses, what the heck. But everything seemed okay. And afterwards I couldn't even seem to hear it anymore. I just got filthy — I'm sorry."

Alice wrapped a towel around his hands and pulled him toward her. "Poor thing." She kissed him with her eyes open. "Oh!" She pushed away.

His face went hot. "What?"

She touched his cheek to make him tilt his head. "Look at yourself," she said, motioning into the mirror. "Your neck."

Jake released a long breath. "You scared me. I thought you'd found an open wound." He wet a cloth and leaned over the sink to rub his neck clean.

Alice slipped her arms around his waist from behind. "My bold, courageous auto mechanic!"

Jake bared his teeth into the mirror. "Yes! Grr!"

She brought her hands up to his chest. "Welcome home from the war, darling," she said into the back of his shirt. Her eyes twinkled just over his shoulder.

"Thank you, dear; I'm glad I survived." He wrung out the cloth and stood straight.

Alice's hands slid down to his trousers. Her fingers pushed into his thighs.

"You know, I have hardly anything at all under way for dinner," she said, her words sliding. "I think there ought to be some reward for the conquering hero."

He heard her let out a small, sharp breath as she moved one hand toward the middle of him. He smiled and intercepted her hand. He lifted it to his face and kissed it.

"Actually, I feel so grimy, I better just bathe before dinner."

"Aw," Alice pouted.

He turned and pecked her forehead with his lips. "I regret it already," he said as he slipped through the doorway.

Stupid, stupid! he growled inside his head as he stepped into the shower. The hot water hissed at him. *You ass – taking such a chance. And what for? Never again.*

Something that smelled wonderful was sizzling noisily when he turned the faucets to "off." By the time he was toweled dry and dressed, the table was set. Alice enjoyed cooking new things; for the first time in her life, there was money for unusual ingredients. She was invariably a superb dinner companion, able to talk but eager to listen. She read the newspaper every day and the *New Yorker* every week and books constantly, and thereby had a steady stream of news and opinions and questions. She was fond of the tongue-in-cheek humor of George S. Kaufman — the only woman Jake could ever remember who was fond of George S. Kaufman; she said he reminded her of Jake. She could be funny in her own right as well — she had a sense of the ironic, and a keen eye for foolishness — yet she magically avoided demeaning people, even when she was laughing at them. She could recount the arrival of a demented homeless man at the mission — a fellow convinced he was to receive an award from President Truman — and she could redden with laughter at her own impersonation of the poor soul; yet she would still somehow communicate her view of him as, indeed, a poor soul. She often ended up wiping away her laughter tears and saying, "The dear! What a dear!" Jake was amazed at how she loved people, and loved helping people in need, yet didn't take any of it seriously enough to become pompous or self-righteous or stuffy.

And Alice had an automatic sense of what was interesting and what wasn't, so she brought exactly the correct mixture of daily go-ings-on home from the mission. Plus, if she did not thoroughly enjoy hearing about the manufacture and sale of bathmats and nipples and doorstops and however many miles of tubing, Jake never got that impression. By her questions and interruptions — "Can they actually afford to keep making that size if they don't replace the Troy account with someone just as lucrative?" — she seemed genuinely involved and interested in Jake's work. Her face and hands were alive when she talked — not overpowering, but animated, engaging. He loved to look at her. There was an open kind of brightness about her that warmed him and delighted him.

They finished with coffee. Jake resolutely commanded his guilt away. *Never again.*

"Alice Valentine, I was lucky to get you," Jake said.

She leaned on the table and propped her chin in her hands. "Like me a lot, do you?" she teased.

"Yup."

"Hm," she responded, closing her eyes. "Come show me."

He stood and took her by the hand. They walked into their bedroom, and he turned to take her in his arms. He liked the feel-ing of his hand on the back of her head as they kissed. He could feel her pushing, her teeth closing delicately on his lower lip, then on his tongue.

"Like me a lot, do you?" she repeated.

They began to unbutton each other but grew impatient and ended up undressing themselves. Alice was on her belly, stretched out across the bed, when Jake turned around.

"My dear," he observed, "I do believe you are trying to seduce me."

"My dear," she replied, ogling his naked body, "I do believe we're already well beyond seduction."

He laughed and knelt on the bed beside her. He was still thrilled by the long lines of her body. They lured his hands into lazy caresses of her skin. Her bottom and thighs were tight and strong from her daily walks; she rarely wanted to drive to the mission. He could kiss her neck and feel the entire length of her back bending like a reed to meet him. He took her by her hips and rolled her over. Her breasts were small and firm; he closed his lips on one of her nipples and tugged gently. With his tongue, he could feel it standing up in a point.

Alice groaned and dragged her nails across the middle of his back. Jake moved his face to the other side of her and let his teeth barely scrape her other nipple. Alice released a kind of complaint and placed a hand at the back of his neck. Jake looked up at her.

"Did I hurt you?"

"No."

But she did not let him go back. With one hand she steered his hips until he moved first one of his knees, then both of his knees, between her legs; with the other hand she pulled his face up to hers. She kissed him deep and guided him into her. The sensation of her long legs brushing against his skin as they wrapped around him sent shock waves through his body — every time. He began to glide in and out of her, with her hips answering his rhythm. With each thrust she gave a little cry, yet her hands on his backside kept pulling him closer, deeper. Her hunger for him made his thoughts reel around in his head, faster and faster, until he could only take her and take all of her and keep taking her, and she erupted in a wringing explosion, and her beautiful anguish made him explode too.

And when they had caught their breath, and he tensed his muscles to pull away, she still held him fast. Her inner thighs clung to him, and her fingernails were settled in the fleshy orbs of his buttocks. She closed her lips on his ear lobe, then let go without moving her mouth far from his ear.

"Shall we have a baby?" she whispered.

Jake got up on his elbows and looked in her face.

"I — Are — Do——"

"This sounds like our first date."

Jake sputtered. "Well — Alice! I — Yes!"

"Oh, good." She wrinkled her nose.

Jake's body suddenly jolted away from her. "Are you — Are we——"

"Pregnant? No!" Alice squealed. "I didn't mean now. I just meant, Should we try."

"Oh." Jake sank into the mattress.

"Aw, I'm sorry, love," Alice said, stroking his face. "I didn't mean to disappoint you." She wrinkled her nose again and grinned. "But this is lovely, seeing you want it."

"What do you mean, 'Should we try?' Haven't we been trying all along?"

Alice plumped a pillow under head. "Not exactly. I've cleverly arranged to be particularly uninspiring during the most critical passages of time." The gleam in her eyes said she was enormously pleased.

"You," Jake howled, rising on his elbows and snaking toward her, "don't know how to be uninspiring!" He gave her nipple a noisy slurp, and she giggled and pulled away, but only for a moment.

6.

Claudette Briscoe was Mr. Fivecoat's matronly secretary, and had been from the formation of the company. But she got sick, missed a month of work, and died on a Tuesday morning.

On Friday Jake stood in a sea of black wool at Haven of Rest Memorial Gardens.

"You don't have to go," Jake had said to Alice.

"I don't mind going," Alice said, "if you think Mr. Fivecoat would want me there."

"There will be a thousand people there. Claudette Briscoe was an institution. Relax. Fivecoat won't know and wouldn't care whether my wife is there or not."

The grim monotone of the graveside service made Jake's brain flicker. He ticked off the items on his schedule for the day, then for the next day. He noted the scuffs on the toes of his black shoes and calculated the time before shining would no longer do and new shoes would be required. He scanned the crowd for Leland Supply employees, counted them, then counted the entire crowd and calculated the percentage of Claudette Briscoe's life that had been consumed by her work.

There was Cora Jessup. Where was Gordon? A town councilman ought to be here, with so many voters assembled in one place, for free. *Oh, Jake, you should be a politician.* Ha. Maybe Cora's right. How many of Leland's 14,000 people do I already know? It could be great for business. He thought of the Statehouse in Columbus. He had visited once as a little boy. A span of steps, stretching wider than the world, leading up to a stand of eight enormous columns, like friendly soldiers beckoning the boy inside, under the safety of the great squat silo of the rotunda. *Come in, young citizen. This place is your place.*

The minister droned on. Even Mr. Fivecoat seemed to shift restlessly.

Jake looked at the old man. It was a tired face. Was he getting grumpier? Seemed so. "Goddamn politicians," he often snarled. Not just about town council. "Legislature pansies." "Never made an honest dollar." "Regulating us out of business." "Part-timers." "Troublemakers."

Jake clasped his thumbs behind his back and drummed his fingers together. He silently tapped out a tune. He reminded himself not to bolt too eagerly for his car when the service was over.

Even so, when the minister said "Amen," Jake's reverie snapped and he took a half-step to steady himself. Family members tossed their flowers on the coffin, and then the throngs were ambling solemnly away. Mr. Fivecoat slipped an arm around Claudette's grown son, who had come in from Columbus, then turned toward the banks of automobiles at the edge of the cemetery. Jake wondered whether to catch up to him. Give him a quick update on the Troy account. Catch any tidbits, any new leads from the front office. Be the snappy salesman, the favorite corporate son. But a grievous sob echoed from behind them, near the grave, and Jake tramped along alone. Could any conversation about the business be appropriate here? Probably not. Fivecoat was walking with a thin young lady in a long gray overcoat; her black hair fell down her back beneath the requisite funeral hat. He seemed to be engrossed in the conversation with her. Jake plunged his fists into his coat pockets. Nuts. A wasted morning.

On Monday Jake arrived at Leland Supply by eight — his weekly routine. He had learned to roll through the plant and chat up the machine people — they started at seven — pat them on the back, let them know he loved them. "I am the marksman!" he once announced to the mold-presser Mackovic, shouting to be heard over the machinery. "But you — *you!* — make the bullets!"

Mackovic loved it; he threw back his bald head and roared with laughter.

So it had become a ritual. Jake would come clanging in through the double metal doors on Monday morning, legs churning through long strides, hands out to either side to touch the shoulders and arms and hands of the people who made the goods — men and women, white and black; here in the factory, colors ran together. The workers' faces never failed to light up when they saw him. "Jake!" they would cry: the black-skinned Mr. Feagle on the conveyor, the transparent-skinned Mr. Svenson on the trimming machine, Mrs. Geist mixing the dreadful goop, dozens of others. "Valentine!" the Europeans would call out. (Mrs. Epperstein invariably called out, "Jacob Valentine, vhat are you doink!") And Jake would wind up on the far side of the plant, at Korman the foreman's massive wooden desk, and he would wave his arms at the mile-high ceiling fans and yell into the echoing din of the factory: "I may be the marksman!" And the workers would chant back: "But *we* make the *bullets!*" Jake would applaud them heartily, turn to shake Korman's hand formally — Korman rolling his eyes at the ceiling — and dash back out the way he came.

Then Jake would head out to make a short day of sales calls, returning to the plant by mid-afternoon. At three o'clock each Monday afternoon, just as the heaviness of the first day of the work week began to settle on people's heads, Jake would make his rounds of the office personnel in a similar manner — without the bombast and noise, without the final cheer, but with every bit of the charm and power. He would end up outside Mr. Fivecoat's office, drop into the visitor's chair next to Claudette's desk, lean an elbow in toward the roundish grandmother and make his report: "This," he would begin — and Claudette came to repeat the phrase with him — "is a very good place to be."

But now Mother Claudette was gone, and as Jake returned to the offices for his Monday afternoon circuit, he wondered how it would end.

In the main hallway, where he usually began, he did not recognize the backside of the figure ahead of him. It was a woman, walking half the length of the hallway ahead of him. She was moving pretty fast, carrying a small leather portfolio. She was slender but shapely, with high heels that showed off her calves and a gray skirt that hugged her hips. Her hair was long and black, and it bounced a bit off of her back as she walked. She was almost to the end of the hallway when Jake placed the hair — the bouncing hair; he put it into slow motion and laid it against a gray overcoat and he could remember her crossing the scruffy lawns at Haven of Rest with Mr. Fivecoat.

When she turned the corner at the end of the hall, she looked a bit to one side — perhaps she saw him out of the corner of her eye? Jake only got a glimpse of her, but he seemed to take a flash photograph of her before she vanished: her body bent in forward motion, her limbs at angles, one arm flexed forward, the other flexed back to reveal a voluptuous bustline and a tiny waist buttoned into a matching gray jacket, high cheekbones and full lips and an elegant straight nose and big thick-lashed eyes.

And she was gone. Jake slowed for a step — he felt the vertigo of an old impulse. Then he sucked a breath and went on his way, bending around the corner en route to his Monday cheerleading routine.

But there she was again.

Now she was standing still, in the middle of the hallway, facing him but studying her portfolio. Jake slowed down as he approached her, and she looked up.

He was stunned by how accurate his instant photograph had been.

"Can I — help you?" he inquired.

"I do hope so," she replied, and he caught a bit of an accent. "I can't seem to locate Mr. Korman."

"Korman the foreman! I'm so glad it's one I know the answer to. I can be your hero!" He gestured down the hall. "Shall we?"

"Thank you."

He shook her hand on the move. "Jake Valentine."

"I'm Katherine Abbott."

"Are you——"

"British, yes. I've been in this country almost four years, and I nearly think I've lost my accent when I meet someone new who sets me straight."

"It's very nice," Jake said. "Beautiful, really. It suits you, Katherine."

"Oh," she breathed, blushing. "Really."

"What brings you to us here at humble Leland Supply?"

"I'm to be Mr. — actually, I am indeed already — Mr. Fivecoat's secretary." She said it the English way, in three syllables — "sec-re-tree" — but then repeated it American-style, smiling self-consciously, elaborately spacing out all four syllables. "I need to learn to speak properly."

"You sound completely proper to me," Jake assured her. "You'll class up the joint. But a Brit, in Leland?"

She smiled the smile of someone who had told a story many times before. "My sister was a war bride; she came to Columbus with her husband. My father is a diplomat; after the war, he was posted to Washington. I didn't want to stay behind in jolly old England. A fellow here in the area, politically connected — Jessup?"

"Ah yes. Gordon Jessup. Town councilman, but way more powerful than that. Basically runs things in this part of Ohio."

"He met my father, recommended me, la-de-da."

"La-de-da," Jake echoed with a smile.

"And what do you do, Mr. Valentine?"

"Jake. Please. I'm just a humble salesman."

He pushed open the metal doors to the factory. The noise engulfed them. "I'll take you to Korman," Jake yelled, signaling toward the opposite corner of the plant.

"Jake!" the Negro Feagle cried, surprised to see him off his usual schedule.

"Mr. Feagle, I'd like you to meet Miss Abbott, Mr. Fivecoat's new secretary."

"Katherine," she said, extending her hand.

Feagle showed his dirty palms and bowed instead. "Pleased to meet you!"

"Jake!" Mr. Svenson exclaimed, smiling.

Jake introduced them. "She got lost, and I found her!" he roared, his eyes teasing her. "I get to be her hero!"

"Jake!" It was Mrs. Geist.

And so on. Every few paces, another worker lit up to see Jake — and he was delighted to introduce the newcomer Katherine Abbott.

She was not inclined to yell over the machinery. She leaned close to Jake's ear. "It seems you're everyone's hero."

He moved his mouth close to her cheek. "I'm the marksman; they make the bullets." The scent of her skimmed his senses. "Here he is."

They were at the big desk. "Korman the foreman! Look sharp! The front office has sent a spy to check up on you!"

He introduced them, took a step back, and put a hand to his heart. "Katherine Abbott, may God be with you."

She smiled, embarrassed.

"Do you think you can find your way back? I could drop bread crumbs along the way."

"I do believe I'll make it," she laughed.

Jake bowed from the waist. "Your humble servant." And he was off.

"Wow," he said aloud, under the clamor of the machines, before he got back to the metal doors. Then he went through them, and in the quiet of the office corridor he took a deep, long breath. Then it was a whisper: "Wow."

The purchaser at Corcoran was on the phone; he needed to delay their appointment by just an hour the next morning. Jake eyed his calendar. He could have done it.

"Don't think I can, Tony," Jake noted. "We'll have to move it to Wednesday."

* * *

"Help, I'm lost," he whined the next morning as he dropped into the chair next to Katherine's desk.

"Indeed?"

"A customer canceled on me!"

Jake leaned an elbow on the desk.

"Cheeky, wouldn't you say?"

"Actually, I'm trying not to say 'cheeky' anymore," Katherine replied, sorting through a stack of paperwork. "Too British."

"So here I am, at loose ends — and I thought I'd check to make sure you got back all right."

"And here I am, Mr. Valentine. Safe and sound." She did not look up from her work, but she was smiling.

"Oh, call me Jake. This is America. You don't have to start every day with Mr. Valentine and get permission all over again."

"I'll try to keep that in mind — Jake."

"Did you know Claudette, the dear departed, who used to have this desk?"

"I'm afraid I didn't."

"She was about a hundred years old."

"A hundred!" Katherine smirked, replacing one stack of papers with another.

"Yes, may she rest in peace. This is a much more pleasant-looking office now."

Katherine kept working.

"In fact, there's a simple mathematical formula you can apply in situations like this," Jake continued. "If Claudette, for example, was a hundred years old, then the office is, I would say, about five times as pleasant now."

"I see."

"Because you're — I'm guessing here — about twenty years old?"

"I'll be twenty-three in February."

"See?"

She stopped working and looked at him. "Jake."

"Katherine."

"You must have work to do."

"You must break for lunch. Aren't you feeling faint? I'll save you."

"My hero once again. But actually, I'd better not."

"Oh, come on."

"You'd better not," she said.

"I'd better not?"

"Aren't you a married man?"

Jake rolled his eyes. "Oh Lord, I forgot! I must have blacked out."

"That explains it." She still wore a bit of a smile.

Jake sat back in the chair to pout. "I was only suggesting lunch, Katherine."

"I see."

"You do me a great disservice, milady. I am a man of honor."

7.

It was almost like thunder when Deenah fell. Ruby felt the concussion of it in the walls of the house. It was nearly suppertime. Mercifully, the valves of Deenah's heart clamped shut in a single massive crush, and her body lurched forward into the front of the stove. Ruby rushed to the kitchen doorway and stopped, horrified.

"God! Mama!"

She plunged forward and began tugging her mother's crumpled body away from the stove. Deenah was too heavy for her. Ruby expelled a stream of curse words as she pushed herself in under her mother's shoulder, straining to gain some leverage. When the huge corpse finally rolled over, Ruby gasped. Deenah's face, neck, and chest had been badly seared by the sizzling metal. It occurred to Ruby later that she had never cursed before. But she did not feel guilty.

A tall, thin Uncle George from Pittsburgh, his wavy black hair slicked down against his scalp, came to settle affairs. He said he had visited when the girls were tiny. A neighbor in darktown had remembered him, and called with the news. By the quality of his hat and tie, Ruby could see he had means. He paid for the funeral and burial.

The house would revert to the landlord, a white man in Bainbridge. Ruby's only kin in darktown, a cousin named Shirley, had just a one-room house, really only a shack; Ruby couldn't stay there long. Uncle George invited Ruby to come live with him and his wife, an Aunt Lela whom Ruby had never met.

"What about Maddie?" Ruby asked skeptically.

"She needs care," Uncle George said.

"Yes?" Ruby responded.

His mouth twitched under his little mustache. "She needs to go to Finnegan."

"The crazy house!" Ruby howled.

"It's a mental health institution," Uncle George replied evenly. "They're professional people, trained to help people with problems like Maddie's." She glowered at him. "They'll take a Negro. Not many places do."

"Take!" Ruby spat.

"Ruby, please. This is best for her."

"I can take care of her. I've turned sixteen."

"We don't have a place for her. It's important for you to stay in school. She'll be comfortable at Finnegan."

Ruby whirled and walked away. She turned into the bedroom and looked at Maddie, sitting so contentedly, a vague smile on her lips. Ruby's stomach knotted.

"God damn this."

"Where did you learn to talk like that!" Uncle George sniffed, standing behind her in the doorway. Ruby locked her eyes on his.

"From the devil who done this to us," she replied.

It happened fast. The next day, time to go. Ruby dressed Maddie in her long-sleeved white blouse with the big frilly collar and cuffs, and her pale blue skirt. She took Maddie by the shoulders and kissed her.

"Bee, key."

Ruby's throat felt too tight for air. She embraced Maddie; Maddie's long body seemed to bend under the pressure.

Two young white men from Finnegan, one maybe thirty years old, the other younger, pulled up out front in what looked like a milk truck.

"Colored," the younger one said.

"I told you," said the older.

"Okay."

"I told you by the address," said the older. "You don't come this far south for whites."

"Okay."

"How long you been working at Finnegan? Three months? You don't know shit."

"Okay, Everett, okay."

They had Uncle George sign the papers on a clipboard. They walked Maddie to the back of the truck. The doors were already open. There were leather straps hanging on the walls. Her head bobbed lazily as she stepped up.

"Bee, key."

Ruby turned away and crunched her eyes closed. Her face was hot. She felt a tightening, an old twisting, somewhere above her stomach. Alice. She should tell Alice. Everything had crashed in on her so fast. She could never even have gotten to the mission. *Alice! The fox! The goose! The corn!*

Both men climbed in with Maddie. They sat her down on a bench along one side and slipped the straps around her arms, her waist, and her legs. One white man got out; the other one stayed in the back with her. The one who got out closed the doors on them and climbed in the cab and revved the engine and drove off.

The milk truck went to Finnegan. It took three quarters of an hour. It was bumpy sometimes, but Maddie sat contentedly on a bench in the back of the truck. The young white man, with very light blond hair and a cowlick in the middle of his hairline, sat opposite her in a gray uniform.

"Ah, ah," she chanted with a half-hearted smile.

The young man whistled. "Damn. You all right, girlie?"

Maddie closed her eyes. "Mm, mm."

The young man wrapped himself in his arms. "You are a sweet one. Colored! Son of a bitch!"

"Bee, key."

The road jostled them like puppets. The young man flopped to one side, and his eye fell on the clipboard. The paperwork was supposed to ride in the cab with the driver.

"Everett made a mistake," the young man snickered, picking up the clipboard. "Dock your pay, mister."

He eyed the form with mock professionalism.

"Madeline D. Tillmore," he recited. "Madeline, Madeline."

"Mm, mm," Maddie hummed.

The young man whistled low.

"What's the D stand for, Madeline? Dee-ranged?" He cackled at himself and scratched at his cheek. "You are pretty, for a colored girl."

She closed her eyes and burbled. "Ma, ma." She sighed hard. "Binky."

The young man stood to cross over to her, and a dip in the road dropped him clumsily onto her bench. "Whoa! Ride, cowboy!" he called out to cover his embarrassment. He looked at Maddie's profile. He looked at the gentle arc of her chest. "That's the way to travel, Madeline," he said. "All strapped in. You can't go anywhere." He touched her sleeve. "You friendly?"

Maddie did not open her eyes. "Binky," she breathed.

"Damn. I'm feeling a little binky myself."

He reached further and laid his hand against her breast. The road bent and pulled his arm away from her, but then he put it back.

She did not open her eyes. "Ma, ma," she murmured.

"No mama for you," the young man said.

Maddie opened her eyes as he undid the button at her neck. "Look at you," he said. "Oh, yes."

The frilly collar kept getting in his way. It was hard to get the other buttons undone. When the blouse was open, there was a thin, smooth undergarment. It had no buttons.

"Well, damn," he said softly.

Maddie closed her eyes again. "Bee, key."

The young man ran his fingers across the fabric. "Mm, mm, mama," Maddie murmured.

The horn honked, two beeps in quick succession. The truck was approaching the back gate. The young man cursed and began doing up the buttons. Potholes marred the road outside the gate, and the delicate work was ponderous. The truck slowed, and he could hear the metallic complaint of the great old gate as Fredo swung it open. Then the truck began to move again, on smooth pavement now, around the front, toward the main entry to Clement Finnegan Institution.

Everett opened the back doors of the truck. His colleague was unstrapping the patient.

"You forgot the papers back here."

"Shut up. I know that," Everett shot back. He took a step up into the truck and grabbed the clipboard off the bench. Maddie's head wagged as the other one pulled the buckles open. Everett stopped, still hunched over, half in and half out.

"Pretty girl," he said quietly.

"You're telling me."

"Mm, mm," Maddie said. "Bee, key."

"Too bad she's crazy," Everett said, backing out of the truck.

"Bee, key," Maddie said.

"Come on, Madeline," the blond boy with the cowlick said, taking her by the arm.

Maddie stepped out happily. The young men led her past the tall white pillars of the building's face and into the quaint foyer. Beyond it was a sprawling parlor smelling of wood polish. A short, stout woman bustled into view. She wore a black leather bag, a flatter version of a doctor's bag, on a strap over her shoulder.

"Good morning!" she declared in a military tone, her voice high and sandpapery.

Everett had taken the paperwork off the clipboard. The woman took the papers and scowled at them. "No problems. Madeline D. Tillmore." She looked up sharply at Maddie, then switched to the official smile. "Madeline, I am Dr. Pierce. Do you understand me, dear?"

"Binky," Maddie answered.

"You won't get a thing out of her," the boy with the cowlick said. "Madeline, I'll take you to your room," the woman said, tucking the papers into her bag. "Do you understand me?"

Maddie chanted syllables, looking into space.

"Come along," the woman replied, leading Maddie by the arm. The two young men followed. They crossed the parlor and headed down a long hall. There was a musty weight to the air in the corridor. Pierce opened a door into a long, narrow dormitory room, and looked over her shoulder.

"Thank you, boys; you're excused," Pierce stated firmly.

The young men wheeled and left Pierce with Maddie in the doorway. Inside, beds lined the walls. Some were occupied by sleeping women. A bony old woman with one eye drooped shut sat with her legs dangling over the side of her bed. She looked at Maddie and began to quake.

"Colored!" she cried, her voice quavering. "Colored!"

"Hush!" Pierce spat at her. "Georgia, you hush!"

The woman fell silent, but her eye followed Maddie down the aisle between the rows of beds.

"You'll be comfortable here," Pierce said, leading the way to a neatly made bed at the end of the row. "This is our women's wing, of course." She caught Maddie by the shoulders to stop her at the right place. Bland yellow pajamas lay folded on the bed. "It's Sunday, short of help," Pierce said. "Here, I'll get you into your clothes." Her fingers fumbled under the frilly collar, until she grew frustrated and lifted the lapels to see underneath.

"Heavens, girl, someone didn't button you right."

8.

The moment it was over, or so it seemed to Jake, Katherine rolled away and drew up her knees.

"What's her name." It was more a demand than a question.

"Who?"

He was surprised by the irritation in his voice.

"Your wife."

"Alice. Why?"

"Why not."

She got out of bed and went into the bathroom. Even freshly spent, even newly annoyed, she was — her body was — captivating.

She was running water in the sink.

"Come back to bed."

"No." She stepped into the bathroom doorway. She was pressing a wet towel against her throat. "This doesn't feel good."

"Maybe you made it too hot."

"Not the towel!" she spat, snapping it away from her skin. "Shut up."

He said nothing. He kept watching her.

"I hate cheap little hotels."

"This is not cheap."

"I hate hotels."

Jake sank back into the bed. His mind raced. *Never again.* But the charm pushed up from deep inside. "I was a desperate man. Can you forgive me?"

"We'll see. Can Alice forgive you?"

Jake's stomach twisted. *You were stupid. Stay steady.* "She's not in this picture. She doesn't need to be in this picture." He waited for Katherine to respond, but she didn't. *This could get ugly.* "You're not going to bring her into the picture, are you?"

"God, no."

"Discretion, valor."

"Don't worry about me tattling, Jake," Katherine fumed. "I hate this."

He was getting out of bed now. He needed to gain the advantage, somehow. "You don't hate this," he coaxed, stepping behind her. "You like this." He reached around with both hands on her flat belly. "You just hate liking it." *That was a good line.* His hands moved up to cup her breasts. They were heavy, and he moaned with the pleasure of their weight.

She pulled a shoulder away from him. "I have to go," she said.

Jake let go and took a step toward the bathroom. *Dodge this bullet,* he told himself. *And never do this again.*

* * *

In Pittsburgh, living with Uncle George and Aunt Lela, Ruby did not make trouble. From her perspective, it was a huge house. Meals seemed elaborate; there was more than enough food. Aunt Lela was not a woman to smile readily, but she seemed to enjoy buying Ruby new clothes. Sometimes her uncle or aunt would mention a grownup son named Anthony, who seemed to live quite some distance away. But Ruby was the only child in the house. She let Aunt Lela do her hair, she attended classes in the Negro school, she kept to herself.

"You're new. What's your name?" a girl asked, plopping down next to her before class.

"Ruby."

"I'm Helen. Where you come from?"

"Ohio."

"Why?"

Ruby looked at her hands in her lap. "My mama died."

"Oh, I'm sorry."

Helen was full of energy. Too full to stop. "Got brothers or sisters?"

Ruby didn't look up. "No."

"Who you living with?"

"My aunt and uncle live here."

"What street?"

"Elmore."

"I go home that way." Helen brushed her skirt. "I never lived anywhere else but here. What's Ohio like?"

"I don't know." Ruby looked sideways at this bubbly creature. "Is it like this?"

"No."

It was a strange place to live, in a neighborhood of Negroes with money. Whites lived less than a mile away. Regular dark-town Negroes lived down the road in the opposite direction. The streets wiggled, and big trees were growing all around, so to Ruby the lines were not clear.

"This school is so big," Ruby said weakly. "And clean and nice. A real toilet."

Helen leaned in. "You lived in the country?"

Ruby half-smiled. "I don't know. Not the city."

"Wanna get ice cream with me after school?"

Ruby's eyes widened with astonishment. "Ice cream!"

Helen giggled. "You know what ice cream is, don't you?"

Ruby smiled sheepishly. "Yes, but I got no money for ice cream."

Helen patted her hand. "I'll make it a welcome-to-Pittsburgh present."

Helen chattered all the way to Dangle's, the ice cream parlor. Ruby tried not to stare as they walked. A Negro barber leaned in his doorway, jawing with a couple Negro men seated on a bench in front of his shop. "Don't stop for him, even if he calls out to you," Helen sneered. "He always wants to tell you a joke, and it's never worth the time it takes." Through the window of a clothing store, Ruby could see Negro clerks serving Negro customers. "My big sister used to work there," Helen instructed, pointing. "Maybe I'll work there someday." Bars and diners and grocery stores. A tailor: "His wife got a divorce from him last year, guess why." Shoe repair: "They say his son in New York is funny, you know, like a girl." Ruby had never seen Negroes doing business, Negroes coming and going everywhere, as if they belonged here.

"We can walk home together every day if you want," Helen suggested brightly. "I live just past you."

"Thank you," Ruby replied softly. "Thank you for the ice cream."

* * *

She got the address for Finnegan, and on Friday evenings she wrote to Maddie. She recorded the week's events, her experiences at the colored school, her impressions of Uncle George and Aunt Lela. Ruby knew that Maddie couldn't read her letters; she could only guess whether someone would read them to her — a nurse? another crazy person? Perhaps some insane person would tear open her letter, then stand on a bed and pretend to read it aloud — babbling nonsense like Maddie.

But Ruby kept writing anyway, her heart aching to make the reach. Each Friday evening, for nine weeks, she sat at Uncle George's desk with Aunt Lela's permission and carefully scrawled the words onto paper. She was allowed to get an envelope out of the proper desk drawer. When she had sealed the letter in the envelope and addressed it, she laid it on the corner of the desk with Uncle George's mail. Each Saturday, he went to the post office in town.

Aunt Lela demanded few words, and Ruby rarely spoke. But after the seventh letter, Ruby could feel a change in her own voice. By the ninth letter, the air was coming out of her differently.

* * *

"Ruby!" Helen exclaimed, across the booth at Dangle's. "You sick? You cough all the time."

Ruby brought a spoonful of ice cream to her mouth but stopped short and coughed. "I know. I'm sorry."

"Don't be sorry for me." Helen pushed her spoon in. "You need to go to a doctor." She sipped her hot chocolate. "It's probably that cold ice cream."

"I like—" Ruby began, then coughed — "ice cream."

"It's January! Look at that." Helen nodded toward the picture window. "Across the street."

The door of a bar was swinging erratically, with a large man hanging onto its edge. He stumbled a step, clung to the door as it moved under his weight, and stumbled another step. His head swiveled as he worked to regain his balance.

"He's a drunk," Helen said in low tones. "He used to be a baseball player but now he's a drunk."

Ruby coughed and frowned at the man as his body moved in all directions. He was big enough to be Raymond, with a huge frame, but under wrinkled, filthy clothes far too flimsy for a Pittsburgh winter. The muscles in her neck closed around her throat, and her face felt hot. What she could make of his face was a different face from the one she couldn't stop remembering — grayish, with sags under the eyes, and a slack mouth. He managed to steady himself by leaning against the doorpost, leaving the door to swing in the wind and smack against the building. A silent, knife-like scream shot through Ruby's brain. Her body jolted on the bench. She slid her legs out of the booth and planted her feet on the floor.

"What," Helen said.

Ruby stood and headed for the door.

"Where you going?" Helen called after her. "You left your coat!"

Ruby pushed the door open and took a few steps to the curb. The air slashed at her skin, but her body was hot. Traffic rattled and roared back and forth in front of her, steam and smoke puffing and fading. Between vehicles she watched the man pull himself off the wall and begin putting one foot clumsily in front of the other, yanking himself along the sidewalk, one hand, sometimes two, on the walls of buildings to steady himself. People walking along the sidewalk made their way around the spectacle.

"Ruby, what you doing?"

Helen was standing beside her, bundled up and holding Ruby's coat.

"You know his name?" Ruby asked without turning toward her.

Down the street, a car horn honked. "I don't remember."

"Raymond," Ruby said, still staring at him. Her throat was on fire. "His name's Raymond."

"You know him? He's so nasty." Helen touched her elbow. "Come on, finish your ice cream."

Ruby pulled away and started walking toward the corner.

"Ruby?" Helen called, but she didn't follow.

Ruby's eyes darted through traffic, looking for an opening. Her heart thumped insistently. At the first opening, she pushed off the curb and headed diagonally across the street toward the man. He was staggering to stay on his feet, steam rising from his face. Suddenly she was at his side. He had almost reached an entryway. He was groping his way to the doorknob. In Ruby's head, a million children wailed. Maddie's body was folding under the impact, floating through the dust, settling to the earth, lying in the dirt, bent like a felled deer. And there was Raymond, hunched like a ghost over her body.

In the doorway, his knees seemed to give way, and he dropped to all fours on the concrete, melding into Ruby's vision. He gurgled and drooled. Ruby stood still and watched as he breathed in steamy spasms, his shoulders heaving, his head hanging.

"You Raymond?" she said softly, against the backdrop of street noise.

He swung his head up and squinted at her. His hair was greasy, his skin cracked leather, slimy and whiskery. Globs of white clung to the corners of his mouth. The stench of his breath made Ruby's eyes water.

"Who you?" he finally replied, his mouth hardly moving.

"You hurt my sister." Her voice was steady.

Raymond's face twisted, one eye closing more than the other. "Huh?" he grunted.

Ruby felt tall, looking down at the man on his knees. She could spit on him. She could kick him. Hit him. Hurt him. She could lunge into him and pummel him with her fists. He could never defend himself. "Hit her with a baseball."

A gust of wind cut between them, and his eyes gleamed yellow-ish. His mouth froze in place. Then his head fell, his face toward the sidewalk. "Jesus," he gasped.

He slumped to one side, toward the building, drew himself awkwardly into a sitting position, his back against the wall. His knees were up, angled out, his arms extended between them.

"I'm sorry," he breathed. "I don't——"

His teeth suddenly showed, his lips pulling back in a grimace, and his eyes clenched. A sob erupted, a puff of stink and steam.

"God!"

He lowered his face between his arms, and his body began to quake.

Standing over him, Ruby felt a brake inside. In the shoulder, in the elbow, in the wrist, in the fingers, in the part that bends and reaches and touches someone who's crying. She felt the shadow of that impulse, but something else reached up from within, snaked around it, coiled it tight, held it back. She felt her mouth go dry.

Raymond stopped himself from weeping, pulled his head up from between his arms just enough to look beyond his hands to the curb. Ruby could see moisture in the wrinkles around his eyes, like twinkly daggers.

"I's raised a Christian," Raymond slurred. "But playin' ball, I strayed. I loved that so much. I got all proud."

His face contorted again. He hid his face between his arms to bite back another sob. He looked up at Ruby again, his skin glistening.

"Two years ago, I never had a drink before."

Ruby stared at a thin, jagged red line cutting through one of his eyeballs. It wasn't pity she felt. It was something else, but she couldn't place it.

"Hittin' that girl," Raymond said, shaking his head. "Your sister." He looked away. "Jesus, I'm sorry." His lips came together tight. He pulled in a breath and looked back at Ruby, his face melted with grief. "What happened to her?"

Ruby didn't move. She hated the sight of him, but her eyes wouldn't let him go. They drilled through him. "She's in the crazy house."

Raymond took in the news for a second, then winced. He dragged one elbow up onto a knee and held his forehead. Tears spilled out of his eyes.

"Ain't we all," he gasped. "I am."

Ruby kept staring. A lump gathered in her throat, but she hated it.

He reached up behind his head and knocked his knuckles on the door. "This my place, right here." His arm dropped back down beside him, and he looked aimlessly down the street. "My crazy house is in my head," he slobbered.

Ruby's eyes began stinging, and she bit the inside of her lip. "I gotta go."

Raymond leaned to one side and let out an animal snort as he tried to push himself up. "Me too," he said.

Inside, Ruby felt the brake release. She called out to herself to stop, but she reached out her hands and clasped his upper arm. She took a step and bent her knees to get some of her weight under him. Even so shrunken, he was much too heavy for her. He struggled to raise himself off the concrete, pushing his elbow against the wall behind him, awkwardly maneuvering his feet. Ruby felt his weight roll back and forth, onto her and back off again, as he scissored and bowed his legs into position.

"Jesus," he muttered as he finally stood, leaning against the building and breathing hard. "Thank you."

Ruby was breathing hard too. She looked into his eyes again, but no words formed. She turned away and started walking up the sidewalk. She watched for an opening in traffic and crossed back toward Dangle's. Helen was standing out front in her coat, crunched up against the cold, her face criss-crossed with confusion and worry, Ruby's coat stuffed under one arm. As Ruby approached, she opened the coat and pulled it over Ruby's shoulders.

"You want to go back in?" Helen asked. "You didn't finish your ice cream."

"No more ice cream," Ruby responded, her face grim. She turned toward Elmore Street. "I don't want no more ice cream."

* * *

"Flowers?" She put down the *New Yorker* and jumped up.

"You have incredible powers of observation, my dear."

She took them and smelled them. "What's the occasion?"

"It's Wonderful Wife Day. All the husbands of wonderful wives are bringing them flowers today."

Alice kissed his cheek. "So it was an obligation. I see." She nipped at his ear lobe. "All right, I hate you."

Jake hung up his jacket as she retrieved a vase. "Somehow this is not how Wonderful Wife Day is supposed to turn out."

"Oh well," she called from the kitchen. "It's not over yet. Maybe there's hope for you."

"I could try to redeem myself by taking you to the movies."

"That sounds like fun." She was snipping the stems. "What's playing?"

"I don't know." Jake stirred gin. "Maybe I just want to show you off."

"I don't think so," Alice mused. "Probably all the husbands of wonderful wives are taking them to the movies tonight. I would hate to be typical."

"Oh well." He sat with his drink in the living room.

She appeared from the kitchen with the flowers in a vase. "These are beautiful." She situated them on the dining room table.

"Glad you like them." He took a sip.

"Now, let me ask you," she began, coming to him. "Do you really——" and she hiked her skirt to straddle him on the chair.

"You'll spill this." She took it from him and set it on the *New Yorker*.

"You'll wreck your magazine."

"Don't care." She snuggled her knees into the chair on either side of him. "Do you really want to go to the movies?"

Jake grinned. She put the tip of her nose against his. "Uh, well, what if I actually do?"

"But I think it's time." She tilted her head a bit and let her face drift forward, until her mouth came to him. It was a warm, open kiss.

Jake pulled back a little. "Time?"

"Mm-hm." She kissed him again.

Now he straightened his neck and crimped his forehead at her. "Time for what?"

"I think it's a good time to get together," she said gently. "If you want to make a baby."

Jake looked at the ceiling.

"Oh, that!" he laughed.

Alice straightened up on his lap. "What! 'Oh, that.' You beast."

He made a crooked smile. "You're just using me! I *am* a beast! Please!"

She crunched herself down close to him. Her fingers scratched at his nipples through his shirt. Her face was close again. He could feel the warmth of her breath on his chin.

"All the husbands of wonderful wives are making love to them this evening."

"Before dinner?" he blurted. "I don't think that's part of the tradition." He scooped up his drink. "Let's eat, and go to the movies, and then I'll see what I can do."

Alice nuzzled his neck. "Before *and* after."

His back stiffened. "You're going to spill this."

"I don't care." She reached between her straddling legs to feel him. "Where are you?"

"An exhausting day as the great American salesman, bringing home piles of money, and flowers — flowers! And a fellow can't be a little tired?"

Alice pushed out her lower lip. "Hmph!" She wiggled back off of him and stood up. She pointedly brushed her skirt. "I have humiliated myself for no good reason." She pecked his cheek again. "Okay, old man, dinner and a movie."

She turned for the kitchen. Jake took a deep drink.

* * *

It was a short drive. "I have an idea," he said. "To run for office."

Alice's face jerked. "What on earth!"

"Fivecoat keeps complaining about these guys. They don't understand business."

Alice's mouth was open. "Honestly, I never imagined you on the town council."

"Not town council. The house. In Columbus."

"Columbus? Jake!"

"I thought about town council, but those guys aren't going anywhere. I talked to Gordon Jessup. His wife is one of my customers. He's on town council, but he's more. He's an old-time strong man around here. Nice guy. He says there's going to be an opening next time around. Parrish is going to run for state senate."

Alice's features were bent with worry. "But Columbus."

"It's not full-time work. I would keep my job." He turned the steering wheel. "We wouldn't move." He glanced at her, then back at the road. "It's just a bunch of meetings."

Alice faced forward and slumped back in the seat. "I never thought of such a thing."

"I know. Me neither. But look at our district. It's basically the county. It's my territory. I know everybody."

The LaSalle eased to a stop.

"I think Fivecoat would love it."

"Well," Alice said, without finishing.

"I think I could win."

Alice opened her door. "I guess I," she began. She stepped out and closed the door. Jake was coming around the car. "I don't know what to say."

"It's a long way off. I would have to talk to a lot of people about it." Jake's eyes crinkled into a smile. "Let's say it's something to think about," he said, sing-songy, and took her arm.

It was Fred and Ginger, reunited, in *The Barkleys of Broadway*. In color! Columbus faded away. Alice squeaked with delight and squeezed Jake's knee. He put his arm around her.

At home in bed, they made love without talking. Alice fell asleep with her arm across his chest. Jake's mouth was dry, he wanted water, but for a long time he didn't stir. Her breathing was feathery. Her shoulder barely moved. He watched her elbow rise and fall as it lay across him, a slow, awkward pendulum opposite her own body's rhythm. He watched for the lazy tempo of his own breaths to coincide with hers. Finally they joined, her shoulder and arm rising together and sinking together, and then tilting gently away from each other again.

* * *

The house still smelled of pine, even without the tree. Pine and cardboard. The ornament boxes.

"I do wish we could have left it up longer," Alice said, swishing the broom.

"I know, me too," Jake replied, manning the dustpan. "But it was a good tree. It served us well. It just got so dry so fast." He dumped the needles into the waste can. "Christmas is a messy holiday."

Alice smiled. Three little bells on the window sill went into a carton. "And so, I guess, our first Christmas is officially over."

"Where does this go?" He pointed to a small box, wrapped in red, on the lamp table.

Alice frowned. "I don't really know. It was for Ruby."

"Ruby?"

"A girl I know. She was coming to the mission every week or so. I kept thinking I'd see her before Christmas. I finally just brought it home. She never goes this long without stopping in."

"So, leave it here? Put it somewhere?"

Alice stood still, her frown deepening. "I should check on her. I've thought of it a few times, but I kept assuming she'd be there the next day."

Jake picked up the waste can and headed for the back door. "What's in the box?"

"It's a goose."

He turned back to her. "A goose?"

Alice picked up the box and stared at it, brow furrowed. "Yes, a little brass goose."

"I'm sure there's some explanation I don't really need."

She looked up at him, but her eyes were focused somewhere else. "The fox, the goose, and the corn?" she said, in a hollow way. "You know?"

9.

Some were violent; some were dangerous simply because they were so active. One man flapped his arms whenever he walked. He had seemed safe enough at first, but he blindly slapped other patients and knocked over lamps and cracked his knuckles on walls as he flew by. He agreed to stop flapping his arms, but continued. He agreed to be more careful, but couldn't. So he was moved in with the "actives."

But these were in the minority, and they were kept in a separate part of Finnegan's main building. A few of the actives had rooms of their own, walls puffy with rugged upholstery. The upholstery was not entirely practical, however. Even the birdman broke his wrist in a room of his own. And there was a limit to how many rooms could be occupied by individual patients. So for the actives who had to be restrained, one large dormitory served as the "cage." Patients there, men and women together, in similar dull yellow pajama uniforms, were strapped to their beds or tethered to the walls, depending on the time of day. To feed them, exercise them, or take them for bathing, workers dealt with only one patient at a time. Some actives required two attendants working together.

There was conversation, of a sort, in the cage. Patients were free to talk, at any rate. But anyone who became abusive and refused to reform was fitted with a gag, the "thong," a hard rubber slab fixed in the mouth and fastened around the patient's head by a thick leather belt. For those who resisted ferociously enough to wiggle the belt free, there was a hooded variety.

But the cage was a world away. By and large, Clement Finnegan Institution was quite naturally placid, worthy of its history. The main part of the building had gone up in the early 1800s, all elaborate molding and wood floors and high ceilings, the mansion of a pioneer entrepreneur. A business collapse led it to become a college, which also failed, but only after a boxy addition had been built onto the rear, along with smaller outbuildings. Then for a while it served as a jail. But the lovely details around the edges of the ceiling, the frames of the doors and windows, the beautiful touches, had miraculously survived. When the state needed a place for the insane, the price was right, and no major restoration was needed. In some parts of the building, where residents would need to be strictly managed, the bars on the windows were already in place.

Most patients passively proved their docile trustworthiness to roam free in the common areas of the building and, during certain times, outdoors. Thus the Finnegan community observed a drowsy routine of sleeping and eating, bathing and whatever passed for recreation. Some could sleep safely without tethers. Some had to be fed; most could feed themselves. Some had to be bathed, and a few could be trusted to bathe themselves; but most fell into the category of patients able to bathe themselves only with supervision, constant instructions and reminders.

Free time, which was most of the time, was occupied by the singular pursuits of the insane. Most of the patients spoke little or not at all. Four typically played cards, although one always required two chairs in order to receive silent advice from the ethereal Captain Knickerbocker. There was a wall of bookshelves, and one young lady was working her way through the collection by a laboriously unconventional method: after turning a page on her lap, she would set the book on the floor, walk completely around it, sit back down and retrieve the book. An elderly man and woman regularly strolled together, she charming him with reminiscences of places she had never been. "I adored Calcutta. I would go back."

At night, most slept. Some roamed. A few minders, and a few maintenance people, could be found in the halls. If a patient was lost, or disoriented, or was one of those not authorized to wander at night, a maintenance worker might let a minder know, and a minder might find the patient, and steer the patient to bed. Or not.

Everett worked at Finnegan each summer during high school and then decided to stay on full-time rather than try college, even though he was generally assigned the dirtiest and most unpleasant duties. Other workers at his level came and went with great enough frequency that he was gradually able to acquire some semblance of authority, by which he sloughed off the worst of the tasks on the newer help. He had mopped up enough urine and feces; he had slopped a soapy sponge on enough dull-eyed "mentals." He was big enough and strong enough to wrestle the actives when they needed it — that was fun, although it rarely happened. But the boring stuff? If they would hire more blacks on maintenance, things would be better. Until, then, let Perry, that new fellow, numb his brain sitting in the paddy wagon with the latest arrival. He was going to drive the damn truck from now on.

There was a table in the kitchen, with cigarette burns in the finish. Somebody always moved the ashtray. Everett looked around and decided on a coffee-ringed saucer, which he slid toward the middle of the table.

"Want one?"

"Sure."

Each took a drag. Everett yawned noisily. "What a job."

"I never thought I'd wind up in the crazy house."

Everett pulled hard on the cigarette. The words came out in smoke. "How'd you get here?"

Perry shifted a bit in his chair. "Let's just say my family's all crazy. Back in Missouri. My dad, maybe he already got the gas chamber. My mama ran off long before. I've wandered a bit."

Everett took another drag. "I don't even think about it."

"Think about what?"

"About it being a crazy house. I been here so long, I actually forget."

"Are you kidding?" The cowlick in the middle of his hairline seemed to make a little yellow flame of his hair. "Raker thinks he's a porcupine. Gormish talks to the doorknobs."

Everett yawned. "I've seen it all, I guess. It all runs together." He drew on the cigarette again. He could not even remember this new kid's name. "It bother you?"

"Bother me? Hell no."

"Well, I guess that's good."

The boy with the cowlick tapped his cigarette nervously on the saucer. "Sounds crazy, I guess, but I like it."

Everett arched an eyebrow. "Well, that's sweet!"

"I mean, it's like a movie. They're all these characters. But you get to know them. Talk with them."

"Sure," Everett said.

"It's like you're in the movie with them. You say something to them, you do something to them, they just keep being the character in the movie."

Everett didn't say anything. Perry leaned toward him over the table.

"Don't you feel like you could start screaming or jumping up and down or shoot a gun, and they'd all just keep right on playing cards and walking in circles and talking gibberish?"

Everett stifled another yawn. "I guess so. Ain't that why it's so boring?"

Perry sat back. "You could call a guy a son of a bitch, what would he do about it? You could kick a guy in the ass, he would hardly know. You could grab a lady's tits, she'd never tell. It's like some other world! Amazing!"

Everett crushed his cigarette into center of the saucer. "Stick around a few years, kid. See if you still think it's amazing." He was standing now. "Get going, time to check toilets, new guy."

* * *

Alice guided her Ford over the gravel streets of darktown. She had rarely been in this part of Leland. It was a brilliantly clear winter day, and the sunlight showcased the faded, peeling paint on the houses. No one was outside; it was too cold. At every corner she scrutinized the street sign, trying to dig out of her memory the name of Ruby's street. Or had she not told her? It was like a million years had gone by. Harrison Street, no. Tyler Street, no. Polk Street.

Yes.

Alice turned the car and let it crawl along the road. She moved her face side to side, hoping to find someone in a doorway, a window, anywhere. When she suddenly saw a man beside a house, rolling a garbage can, she put on the brakes. She hurried to roll down the window before he could get away.

"Excuse me!" she called. He didn't look up. Cold air swooshed into the car. Louder, then: "Hello!"

The man stopped and looked. His face opened with surprise, but just as quickly closed again.

"I need some information," Alice called. "Only some information. Can you please help me? May I talk to you?"

The man paused, then set the garbage can square on the ground. His jacket was too lightweight for such weather. He glanced up and down Polk Street, then started walking toward the car, favoring his right leg. He had a fringe of gray hair around a bald head, a splash of black freckles across his cheeks. He was blowing steam from his nostrils.

"I'm sorry to bother you," Alice began before he had reached her. "I'm looking for the Tillmore residence."

The man halted a safe distance away.

"Tillmores? Do you know them?"

He wasn't saying anything.

"I'm not — there's no — no trouble. I just have a gift for Ruby." She turned away, took the little red box from the passenger seat, and held it up in the window. "We're friends."

"Tillmores gone," the man finally said, his voice low. "They cousins maybe help ya. They over there." Alice looked where he was pointing, on a diagonal across the street.

"Thank you so much," she replied, bringing the box back in and taking hold of the window handle. "I really appreciate your help."

"If it's collections, don't bother," the man added. "No money there."

"No! I'm just a friend, really. Thank you again."

The man stood still as she rolled up the window and pulled away. She rolled into place in front of a tan shack, roof sagging, missing half a window frame.

At the front door, she knocked twice, a bit tentatively, but the door rattled anyway. She pulled her coat collar closer to her neck and looked back over her shoulder. The man across the street was gone. She fingered the little box in her coat pocket and knocked twice again, harder. The door shook noisily.

"Hello?" she called.

Something rustled inside. A thin curtain at the window swished, then bent away. Part of a dark face appeared in the gap, then the curtain went slack again. Something clacked on the other side of the door, and then it squeaked open just a crack, and the same part of a dark face was visible.

"Hello, I'm sorry to bother you. My name is Alice Valentine. I'm a friend of Ruby's. Ruby Tillmore?"

"Yes?"

"Is this — Are you — family?"

There was no answer.

"I have a gift for Ruby," Alice said, drawing the box out of her coat pocket. "I thought I'd see her before Christmas, but — I don't — She always came to see me. I don't know where she is."

"Gone to Pittsburgh," a young woman's voice said.

Alice inhaled. "Pittsburgh," she repeated. "But — why?"

"You her friend, and you don't know?"

"Well, I — I work at the mission. Ruby came for food sometimes." Alice felt herself struggling but couldn't get steady. "She didn't want me to — she said her mother didn't—"

The face was silent.

"Can I speak to her mother? Or could you—" She held out the box. "Could you give her this, for Ruby?"

The face didn't move.

"Her mother's dead."

Alice froze. "I'm so sorry." She withdrew the box. Her mind was spinning. "What about her sister?"

No reply.

"Ruby said she was sick. Maybe I could leave the gift with—"

"They all gone."

Alice began to speak again, but nothing came out.

"You no friend."

"I'm — sorry, Sorry to bother—"

The face vanished. The door closed. Something clacked again.

Alice slipped the box back into her pocket and turned away. She walked back to the driver's side and got in. She was taking shallow breaths. She pulled the car into gear and slid away.

10.

"So late," Alice murmured, hardly opening her eyes.

Jake was emptying his pockets in the dark. "I'm sorry."

"Where've you been?"

"My last call ran late, over in Pierpoint." He was pulling off his clothes.

"Too late for that," Alice murmured.

"Then I dropped by the office and Fivecoat was still there."

Alice was silent.

"He was ranting about the legislature again."

Alice was staring steadily through the darkness at the clock.

"I told him my idea about running."

"Jake, it's almost ten o'clock."

"I'm sorry! I lost track of the time." He slid into bed. "He wants me to run."

Alice inhaled deeply.

"Come here, I'll kiss you and make it all better."

Alice lay still. Her father growled in the ether. *Come here, sweetie, gimme a little kiss.*

"Hey, I'm sorry I'm so late."

"Is that whisky?"

"Oh. Sorry. Fivecoat had some."

Alice turned away.

"Come on, woman," Jake said playfully. "Gimme a kiss or I'll tickle you to death."

Or I'll beat your ass.

"Aw, come on, Alice, forgive me."

She could hear in the dark, from his voice, he was smiling.

"I'll get home on time from now on. I'll be a good boy. I'm bereft! You don't want to leave me bereft, do ya?"

Want me to go over to Patty's place and get a kiss?

Alice sighed. "Stop it. I'm just tired," she replied. "It's late. Let me be."

Jake dropped onto his back. In the dark, the stillness, as he looked at the invisible ceiling, he talked to himself.

That didn't go very well, did it?

* * *

It was so sunny, and the air so still, it almost felt mild, and people were in the little park downtown, even on a January day. Coming back from post office, Alice decided to sit on her favorite park bench, tucked between two thick trees, facing the sun. She pulled an apple out of her purse. Two women, overweight to the same degree, sat on the other side of one of the trees, out of sight, two benches away.

"Oh, Irene," one said, half under her breath.

"It's true!" Irene answered, almost as quietly. "How long has she been married? And still."

"Well, I don't think you can assume that."

"Well, I do, Mamie, and I told her so."

"Irene! You didn't."

"I did. She was making such a fuss about her beautiful Gracie and Gracie's wonderful husband, and how it must be a medical issue." She snorted. "I've heard about that boy."

"You're terrible."

"I'm not terrible. I'm just truthful, that's all. All I said to her was, 'Carol, if he comes home at night and doesn't have enough left for his wife, why not?'"

"Oh, Lord! Irene!"

"He's running around, no question about that. She should have had six babies by now."

Mamie yelped.

Alice had only taken two bites of the apple, but she wasn't hungry anymore. She stood and headed in the direction of the mission.

"Don't act so shocked," Irene sneered at Mamie. "You know it's true, too."

Alice tossed the apple under a bush as she walked. The crisp air didn't seem to match the blazing sunshine. Her coat was right for the season, but somehow heavy. She felt the damp of perspiration at the back of her neck.

At the mission, she unlocked the door, and stepped inside. She was hanging her coat in the closet when she felt the grinding in her lower back. In the bathroom, sitting on the toilet, she saw the red, a slow, malevolent swirl in the water. Deep inside her, a cramp gathered strength. Her throat tightened, clenched against a sob.

* * *

The LaSalle looked perfect, pulling up in front of Finnegan. The bleached face of the main building was chiseled from the same era as the car. The car puffed steam into the frigid January air, and Jake could see his breath as he headed to the front door.

Inside, he closed the big door against the cold and found no one at a little desk in the foyer, a room like a grandmother's, so he stepped into the parlor. He hadn't known what to expect. For a crazy house, he said to himself, this is quite grand. He took in the paintings on the walls — innocuous landscapes, mostly — and the aged drapes over the tall windows.

"Oh, I'm sorry," a spry middle-aged woman said, her blocky shoes clopping quickly on the wood floor. "I'm normally at the front desk, but — never mind."

Jake smiled warmly. "Don't worry. I just got here."

She touched her hair. "Mr. Valentine?"

He touched her elbow. "You can call me Jake."

"Too much to do, too little time. Let me take you to Dr. Pierce's office."

She headed toward one of two large doorways.

"What's your name, young lady?" Jake asked, following her.

She almost laughed. "I haven't been a young lady for a long time! I'm Erma." She opened the first door she came to. "Dr. Pierce, I have Mr. Valentine here for you." She glanced back at him. "Jake. From Leland Supply."

Jake touched Erma's elbow again as he stepped past her toward the doctor. "Thank you, Erma, for taking care of me."

"I can take your coat, Mr. — Jake."

He slipped it off. "Thank you again!"

Erma was still smiling as she closed the door, Jake's overcoat draped over her forearm.

Dr. Pierce came around her desk and shook Jake's hand. "Hello."

"Thank you for seeing me, Dr. Pierce," Jake began. "I won't take much of your time."

Pierce gestured toward a pair of red leather chairs in a corner. "Sit."

They sat. "We'd like to help you however we can. We want to be good neighbors. Contribute to the important work you're doing here. We produce rubber goods. If we don't make something you need, we may be able to fabricate it. I imagine you may use rubber gloves here."

"Yes, we go through a lot of rubber gloves," Pierce echoed, her face unmoving. "We use a medical supply out of Columbus."

"Of course. I just want to let you know we're available to you. Our prices are always good. We're right here in Leland. With us, you're not paying for a lot of expensive shipping. Maybe I could give you an estimate."

Pierce stood. "All right."

Jake stood, smiling, and reached with both hands. "Thank you for your time."

Pierce didn't smile back. Jake withdrew his left hand and she gave his right a single, solid pump.

"I'll see you out," she said.

"Oh, no need." Jake reached for the door knob. "I remember the way."

"Very well. Good day."

"I'll mail you an estimate. Thanks again."

Jake closed the door behind him and exhaled. Dr. Pierce did not seem to be charmable. He looked up the empty hall. Maybe he would have a look around. Maybe find an opportunity. If someone objected, he could claim he was lost.

Pierce sat at her desk and felt herself deflating. Medical school, for this. But everywhere she had turned, it was one excuse or another. They didn't have to say it; it was all over their faces. *We've never had a woman doctor here before.* Her first job, teaching in Chicago, bored her to tears. Her year in Lemont, trying to be a small-town doctor, was a horror. When Gallagher, the superintendent of schools, got sick, she knew he needed better care. She urged him to go up to Chicago, but he refused. And then, when he died, and Mrs. Gallagher harped all over town about "that lady doctor," there was no recovering the practice. Even coming here, to Finnegan, it was made clear she was on thin ice. "We've never hired a woman to lead this institution," Shaw intoned, in his official capacity as chairman of the trustees. Indeed, since its inception as an asylum, no woman had ever run the place. But her father had pulled strings. So at least, finally, she had a chance to prove herself.

Now, though, it was all funding, funding, funding. Every step was a potential endangerment to the state funding that fueled the operation. Not a single hour of her medical studies had prepared her for this pressure — the byzantine intermingling of money and politics and personalities and history.

She urgently wanted a cigarette. But no. She was making good on that commitment. She could tell, last summer, that her cough wasn't about anything but her habit. And sure enough, the cough had disappeared with the cigarettes. The weight gain was mortifying. She had never been this big. She opened the top right drawer of her desk and took two hard candies, small red balls, and popped them in her mouth. She rolled them around with her tongue. Two at once, she had figured out, kept her mouth better occupied than one.

Still, God, she wanted a cigarette.

* * *

He found Finnegan to be even bigger on the inside than it looked from the outside, with tile-floored hallways that echoed and innumerable identical doors. The occasional orderly appeared pushing a cart of supplies, or a dull-faced person in a wheelchair, but Jake put on a professional face and kept walking. Where doors were ajar, he peeked in. One opened on a broad dormitory, with two rows of beds, and men of all ages lying in them, or sitting on them, or standing next to them, or wandering. At the opposite end of the building, he found another dormitory, this one full of women. One stood facing a corner, her head swinging slowly from side to side, like the pendulum of a clock. Another, skinny and dark-haired, danced a jittery dance in a narrow circle, smiling out of half her mouth and wagging her fingers. A number of them sat on their beds in silence. One, with a square face and feathery hair, her hands folded neatly in her lap, lifted her chin every few seconds and said, "Oh!", then returned to her reverie. An old woman, her bones showing through her skin, sat up in bed as she noticed Jake in the doorway. One of her eyes wouldn't open. She pointed at a brown-skinned young woman, asleep on her back, a couple beds away.

"Colored!" she rasped.

Jake stepped into the room. Among the blank faces, the yellow eyeballs, the wisps of greasy hair, the brown girl seemed utterly out of place. Maddie was breathing evenly, her face resting in a sublime half-smile. Jake could not remember ever seeing a more beautiful Negro girl.

"Can I help you?"

A young man in gray hospital garb was standing next to him. Jake extended his hand. "Jake Valentine. I'm conducting a study, a cost analysis. Looking at the institution's consumption of rubber products."

The young man looked steadily at him.

"I'm with a company in Leland."

"Maybe you should see Dr. Pierce," the young man said.

Jake's eyebrows went up. "I just met with her! We agreed that I would bring her my findings."

"Oh," the young man said. "Well, then." He ran his fingers through his blond hair, pushing back the cowlick in the middle of his hairline.

"I would be grateful if you could help me, young man," Jake said, placing a hand on his shoulder. "I would not expect you to serve free of charge, you understand."

The young man looked into his eyes. "Maybe I can help you, sir."

Jake smiled broadly. "Call me Jake. Yes, thank you. And your name is?"

"Perry Gavin. Let's walk." He moved toward the doorway. "These folks get nervous with visitors."

"Of course." Jake followed him into the hall. "Rubber products. You know, I assumed rubber gloves would be the big thing, but maybe you have other ideas."

Perry led him to another door and opened it into a supply station. "I mean no disrespect, sir, but they call this the rubber house. This place runs on rubber."

He reached into a drawer and pulled out a thick rectangle of rubber. "The polite term for this is *mouthpiece*," he said, handing it to Jake. "But usually we just called them thongs. It goes in the inmate's mouth, whenever you need them to — well, you don't want somebody to bite you. Ties on with a leather strap."

Jake turned the piece over in his hand. It was pocked with teeth marks. One corner was ragged. "How often do you — I mean, how many of these do you use?"

Perry shrugged. "Sometimes ten, sometimes twenty times in a week. I guess you're supposed to throw them away after you use them once, but we try to clean them off afterward."

Jake could see a stream of them coming down the conveyor belt in the factory.

"May I take this with me, Perry?"

"You can do whatever you like." He motioned down the hall. "I think you'll want to see the rubber rooms."

"I think you're probably right," Jake said as they walked.

"I'll show you one that's unoccupied," Perry said. "That will be less unpleasant for you." He stopped at a door with a small window cut into it, and a sliding panel covering it. He took a ring of keys out of his pocket, unlocked the door, and pulled it open.

"The toughest cases, the violent ones, have to go in here."

Jake stepped in. The walls and floors were covered with puffy upholstery. In places, the fabric was tattered, as if it had been chewed by an enormous rodent.

"I thought you said this was the rubber room," Jake said, pushing on the wall, feeling its elasticity.

"It's what we call it," Perry said. "And I think, if I understand your line of business, it *ought* to be rubber."

Jake turned to him in surprise.

"They chew on the fabric. It gets filthy. Moldy. Rubber would last longer. And it would be way easier to clean."

Jake nodded.

"There are five more rooms just like this one. They all ought to be rubber."

"You think like a salesman, Perry."

"Thank you, Jake."

"We could use someone like you at Leland Supply."

"I imagine I would like that very much, Jake."

Jake pulled his billfold from his jacket pocket. "Perry, I want to thank you very much for your excellent help." He looked both directions, then handed over a ten-dollar bill.

Perry's face opened. "This is very generous."

"I think you've performed a valuable service to our company."

Perry pushed the bill into his pocket. "I don't think you'll have any reason to tell Dr. Pierce or anyone about this little tour."

Jake shook his head. "None at all. I'll find my way out, and maybe I'll be in touch with you later."

"Not here. I could write my address for you."

Jake pulled his billfold out again. "Take my card. Write me there."

11.

"You look grim."

Jake looked up quickly from his plate.

"Grim?"

"You're so quiet," Alice said, half-smiling. It was pork roast tonight. He loved pork roast. It couldn't be a problem with the pork roast.

Jake made a smile and took another bite. "Sorry." He chewed. "I went to Finnegan today."

"Oh my, how was that?"

Jake scooped peas onto his fork. "I still don't know."

"Hard to see people in that condition?"

Jake chewed again. "All different conditions. I — I don't know. People who——"

Alice ate and waited.

"Crazy old people. People who can't talk, or just say the same thing over and over again. Or keep doing the same thing. Or — then — there was a black girl. A teenager. Just — I don't know."

"What did she do?"

"She was just sleeping. In the women's dorm." He stabbed another piece of pork. "She was just — everybody else seemed crazy. She just seemed — I don't know. She was beautiful."

"Really." Alice watched him thinking.

"I don't know why it hit me." He poked at the meat. "Never mind," he finally said. "This pork is so good."

Alice giggled. "You always say that."

"It's always true. You've created an addiction."

She wrinkled her nose. "I have you in my power!"

Jake grinned. "Pork power!"

* * *

When Ruby had been coughing a week, Aunt Lela took her for an examination. In Pittsburgh there were doctors for blacks with money. Ten weeks to the day from her arrival in Pittsburgh, Ruby was diagnosed with tuberculosis.

"Tee bee," she heard Aunt Lela explain.

"What does it mean?" Ruby asked.

"It means you're very sick, dear, and to get you well, we'll have to send you away."

Aunt Lela, tight-lipped, packed clothes for her in a heavy trunk. Uncle George seemed stricken himself. Into the trunk he laid one sturdy box containing pale blue writing paper and another box of blank envelopes.

"I've already put a stamp on each of the envelopes," Uncle George pointed out, trying to sound cheerful.

Ruby thanked him, but she shivered as she peeked in at the gift. He had given her a hundred envelopes.

Ruby wrote her tenth letter to Maddie from the sanatorium in Huntsburg. She was too weak to write the eleventh.

* * *

He was in the area, so he stopped at Karney's before heading home. Rory poured gin over ice without asking.

"Jake Valentine," Perry said, three stools away, hunched over a beer.

"Perry," Jake replied, extending his hand. "I got your letter."

"I do hope to hear from you again."

"You might. I've talked to the boss about adding salesmen. So far it's just me."

"Sell anything to Finnegan?"

"Nothing yet, but it will happen. You set me up to make a hell of a proposal."

"I was happy to."

"I've talked with Pierce a couple times. We'll definitely do the gloves. And the thongs. We can make them cheaper. And I think the rubber walls will get approved."

"I've been thinking about what you said."

Jake looked sideways at him.

"You know, I wouldn't mind getting into a different line of work."

"I couldn't blame you. How long have you been there?"

"Just five months. But I have more energy than that. I work a lot of graveyard. There's not enough to do. Finish my work, and sit in the kitchen for the rest of my shift. Read, sleep, whatever." He looked into his beer. "I probably shouldn't be telling you this."

"It's okay," Jake answered.

"It's just that, I think I have more to contribute, you know?"

"Yeah. I know the feeling."

* * *

A cat was in heat, and the screaming woke Everett. He sat up uncomfortably. Asleep on the night shift again. He went to the window and hissed, although he could not see the animal. The night was inky, moonless. He plunked back down. His eyes searched the dark.

The kid must be making the rounds. He still had trouble remembering his name. Perry. Weird kid. Anyway, Everett was happy to hand off the worst of the night shift to him.

He leaned forward and twisted the cap on the bottle. He started to pour, but then he held the bottom of the bottle up to the light. Close to empty. He swigged the last of it.

He closed his eyes, and the gauzy film of sleep began to settle over him. *Gotta bring a fresh bottle tomorrow. No, tomorrow I'm off.* A long, slow yawn overtook him. *Back on Monday.*

* * *

The women's wing was a tomb of sighs and snores. Blankets rose and settled with deathly calm. With his shoes off, the young man could cross the floor in silence, the yellow flame of his cowlick silhouetted in the twilight. At Maddie's bed, he guided a hand under the covers. The pajama buttons were big and easy. She turned toward him and opened her eyes as he groped her, but she said nothing. He drew back the blanket and sheet and pulled her pajama bottoms down around her ankles.

"Damn, is that a bump on you?" he said under his breath. "Damn, I'd miss you."

He didn't hesitate. He pulled on the drawstring of his hospital trousers, slipped in alongside her, and pulled up the covers.

"Fine," he purred, and he took her by her shoulders and turned her away from him. "Yes, that's it, Mama," he droned as he entered her.

He did not take long.

"Mm, mm. Bee, key."

He withdrew and worked fast. He pulled up Maddie's pajamas and buttoned her up. Then he was out of the bed, his own trousers tied up, the covers pulled back up to Maddie's chin.

"Colored!" rasped the bony woman with one eye drooped shut. "Colored!"

Perry tip-toed to her and sat on the edge of her bed. "Georgia, you say that every time," he chuckled. And he kissed her on the forehead before he left.

* * *

Jake reached across to touch her, but she wasn't there. Then he heard the toilet flush, and her nightgowned silhouette appeared in the murky early morning.

"Happy anniversary, beautiful," he said, smiling and extending his hand to her as she approached her side of the bed. "One excellent year!" But she didn't take his hand. She turned away and sat on the edge. Puzzled, Jake lay still, then awkwardly scooted sideways toward her, placing his palm in the middle of her back.

"Hey," he said quietly.

Alice's body moved up and down under his hand. Her head sagged away from him. Then he could hear a high groan, from deep inside her, forced out through clenched teeth, and sharp, wet, inhaling gasps. Jake sprang upright, threw the covers off, and swung around to sit next to her, his arm around her.

"God," he breathed. "What's wrong?"

Alice's face was in her hands. Her sobs began coming faster and shorter, as if her lungs were pounding at her throat. Jake's heart raced. His brain clattered with a tickertape of terrible possibilities.

"Alice, what is it?"

Alice leaned into him, her shoulder in the middle of his chest. Her hands fell into her lap, and she turned her face into the side of his neck. Her sobs disintegrated into a gurgle. Jake reached across and laid his hand on hers.

She let out a long, cavernous sigh, and finally breathed in again with a small shudder. Her voice was a broken warble.

"I started my period."

Now it was Jake's turn to sigh. "Oh, Alice." He wrapped both arms around her and hugging her. "It's okay."

Alice took a sharp breath. "No it isn't." Her eyes crunched closed, and more tears flowed. "I've prayed and prayed to have a baby." Her body shuddered again, and she pressed her face hard into him.

"It hasn't been that long," Jake murmured. "It will happen, babe."

They sat in silence. Alice's breathing grew steadier. She didn't move her head off of his neck. She looked into the dawning gray.

"When?" she whimpered. "Why isn't it happening?"

Jake stroked her hair away from her wet face. "It takes time, sometimes," he said softly. "It will happen."

She straightened a little, and he backed away to look at her face. In the dawn light, he could see the streaks and splotches.

He smiled warmly. "We'll have a good day," he said. "I'll take you to Partridge's."

Alice couldn't help but grin. "Big spender." She sniffed.

"Cherry Coke," Jake said. "I think maybe it was just something in the Cherry Coke that made you fall for me that day."

Alice reached for a tissue. "Yes, it did taste a little funny."

Jake barked a laugh.

She blew her nose noisily. "Sorry," she said. "That was ugly."

"You're beautiful," Jake replied, pulling her close and nuzzling her ear.

* * *

"I do — not — know," Pierce snapped. Everett had seen her angry a million times, but he had never heard her raise her voice like this with Shaw. The chairman of the trustees rarely showed up, and when he did, everyone was on their best behavior. In the corridor, Everett leaned a shoulder against the wall near Pierce's door. Shaw's voice was too low for him to make out the words.

"As best we can," she argued. "We can't make it a military base."

More Shaw, garbled.

"I know that, of course."

Shaw.

"A patient, I assume. Heavens, Dr. Shaw. *Staff?*"

Shaw.

"Six months or so. Her health is good."

Shaw rumbled a long time now.

"A sister, and an aunt and uncle. In Pittsburgh."

Shaw again.

"No, they released her to us unconditionally. But I suppose, if they wanted the child, it would be easier——"

Shaw interrupted her. He talked a long time again.

"All right, I understand."

Shaw.

"No, frankly, I don't agree. I don't like going to Sangamon when there are family members who might——"

He interrupted her again.

"Yes, I understand that concern. I'll contact Sangamon."

"Oh good," said a young nurse, making Everett jump. "I can't find anyone else. We've got vomit in men's."

"Oh great," Everett said. "Where is that kid?"

He found Perry in the kitchen, dozing. He kicked his shoe.

"Glad you're working days for Osgood's vacation?" he snickered. He cocked his head toward the door. "Vomit in men's."

Perry yawned.

"And guess what I just heard in Pierce's."

* * *

It was hot for May in northeastern Ohio. Jake already had his jacket off, draped over his arm. The door closed behind him. He was beaming like a child. Alice's eyes sparkled as she kissed his cheek.

"I can't wait to hear whatever it is!"

"Jessup invited me over," Jake began, sitting at the kitchen table.

"Oh my," Alice cut in, sitting across from him. "This must be huge. You never come home and stop in the kitchen on the way to a martini."

"Listen. Not his office. His house. He twisted his ankle; he's not going anywhere. Nice house, by the way. Very nice house."

"And?"

His eyes were dancing. "Cora was off work early, to help him, I guess."

"His wife?"

"His wife. My customer. Randover Appliance. Anyway, she served us coffee. I knew something was up when I walked in and she didn't even say hello. She said, 'Jake, I *told* you you should be a politician!'"

Alice pursed her lips. "Will you please tell me what happened?"

Jake pushed out a big, emphatic breath. "Gordon's going to back me."

"Oh my!"

"He can't make an announcement yet. He says he's got a few more people to get in line. So it's not something to talk about yet. He was very much playing the big shot." Jake narrowed his voice and pushed it through his nose to mimic the councilman. "I will not give you bullshit, Valentine. With Parrish running for the senate, we don't have another good candidate. We have people who want it, but everybody's got problems. You're so young, you don't have any baggage yet. We can run you as a fresh face."

Alice's eyebrows were high. "What did you say?"

"I said, 'I'll take that!'"

Alice stood, not quite smiling, stepped around the table toward him, touched his face.

"My politician man."

Jake rolled his eyes, grinning again. "Crazy!"

Alice leaned over and kissed his forehead. Then she straightened and turned to peer into the refrigerator. "It does make me wonder, though."

"Wonder what?"

"What problems the others have."

12.

Rory put ice in a fresh glass, poured another gin, and swapped it for Jake's current empty one. Jake swirled it with his index finger.

"It's hot, Rory," Jake mumbled.

"It's July, Jake."

"You know there's such a thing as air conditioning now," Jake replied.

"Talk to Mr. Karney about it."

"I would think you'd want to. You're the one who has to work in this swamp."

Rory kept drying glasses.

"Karney must think we'll be thirstier if he keeps it hot in here."

"Maybe."

"But there comes a point of diminishing returns, buddy," Jake went on. "Eventually it's such an oven, nobody'll want to walk in here."

"I see that hasn't stopped you yet."

"It's like marriage," Jake said.

Rory's face opened wide. "Marriage?"

Jake pulled an ice cube out of his glass and popped it into his mouth. "Never mind," he said, slurping.

Rory turned away. He had chores to do.

Jake looked over his right shoulder, then his left. Summer. Seemed like all the women in the world were dressed for the heat. Sleeveless dresses. Deep, wide-open necklines. Flimsy fabrics, cinched tight at the waist.

He sighed. Two women were sitting at the end of the bar, chatting. The one facing Jake glanced past her friend at him, then back at her friend.

Pretty girl. Time to take action. Cute hair. Make the move. Lovely body. Here we go.

No.

Jake took another drink.

It's not like that anymore. Things change. It's Alice now. Do right. Be a husband. Be good.

The girl talked to her friend, listened, then talked again, then listened again. Jake glanced, then stared into his gin, then glanced again.

Late appointment canceled. Freed him up early. No schedule. Glance.

It's not like anyone gets hurt, if something happens. I mean really. It would be a passing thing. Alice doesn't find out, no one gets hurt. And Alice wouldn't find out. She doesn't have to find out. She won't.

Glance. The girl didn't glance back.

She must be very soft. Very warm, and very soft. Soft, but full of energy.

Geez, Jake, stop this. What is this?

The pull of the possibility. The pleasure of the pull. The power of the pleasure.

God, no. Stop this. This is just your history, clawing at you. Those women in your past. They're past, dope. Past. You're living in the present now. You've got a future. Grow up, goddammit.

Glance.

But the past is still here. With me. In me. It's hanging on me.

The presence of the past. The possibility of the pleasure. The power of the possibility. The pull of the power.

Jake tossed back the last of his drink and put cash on the table.

"Too hot for ya, huh?" Rory smiled.

"Too hot," Jake echoed, spinning away from the girls and heading toward the door.

His hand was on the door handle of the LaSalle when he heard her voice.

"Hey, nipple man."

Jake looked around at Paula Ricard, tossing away the end of a cigarette.

"I was just on my way in," she said with a slight smile. "Buy a girl a drink?"

Jake faltered a bit, taking her in. "I," he began, "was just on my way out."

"So?"

"So, I," he began again, but stopped to take a breath.

Paula moved close to him. "You're so *sporadic*, Jake." She said it in three distinct syllables — *spore, rad, dick* — making her lips shape the sounds, and clicking the end of the word with her tongue. "You're here, then you're gone. I think we need to smooth you out."

"I figured you'd have another boyfriend by now."

Her eyes flashed merrily. "I'll kick him down the lane. I think you're worth it."

She looked very fine, the narrow straps of her halter top angled over her collarbones and disappearing behind her neck.

"I've really got to go, Paula," Jake said quietly. "I gotta get home. I'm sorry."

"Home? Seriously?" Paula replied, reaching to take his hand.

Jake pulled his hand away and put it back on the door handle.

"Yeah, seriously," he said, opening the door. "I gotta get home."

"Somebody new-ew," she sang. "Next girl."

"I have a wife," Jake said drily.

Paula's features flattened. "Wife," she repeated. "When did *this* happen?"

"April."

She tilted her head. "Newlywed! Congratulations."

He turned away a bit. His face felt hot. "April last year."

"You were married? You never said a word! You——"

But he closed the door. She shut her mouth tight and stared at him through the window. The engine rumbled to life. Jake tried to pull into gear gently, not to look panicky, but his foot wasn't steady, and the LaSalle lurched away.

Jake's head was swimming.

"Not a good idea," he lectured himself. "Not a good idea."

His brain was rubbery with gin. He rolled down the window. The July air roared in and gagged him. He clutched the steering wheel and sucked huge breaths, trying to clear his head. The sound of the tires changed as he glided off the road onto the gravel shoulder and back again.

"Not smart."

Reaching the town square was something of a victory. He found a place to park; he shut down the car. He needed to get out, take a walk, get his bearings, before he drove the rest of the way home. *Just a walk through the little park, that's all, then I'll be better.*

The trees were huge scribbles of green, mottling the park with late-afternoon shade. Jake walked as steadily as he could, grateful for a refuge from the sun. He didn't get far before tires crunched to a stop on the street behind him. A car door opened, and he turned to see Paula striding toward him.

"Oh God," he said under his breath.

"You're an ass," she announced. Then she was in his face. "You're an ass."

Jake said nothing. Paula's face flared at him. "Well?"

Jake put his hands in his pockets. He felt his shirt clinging to his skin. He pushed his tongue against the roof of his mouth to move the alcohol around in his brain.

"I'm sorry," he finally said.

"That's bullshit."

Jake took a deep breath and turned sideways, away from her fury.

"What I was," he finally said, "isn't what I am."

"What you are now is an ass," she snarled. "You use people. You're a user. You're just done using me."

She raised one hand and pushed his shoulder. He pivoted a bit to keep his balance. "I'm differ," he mumbled, then licked his lips and tried again. "I'm different now."

He looked into her eyes. They were such pools of black, he had to catch his breath.

"I'm a family man," he said weakly, his brain soggy. "I'm going to be a father. I might run for," and he paused, "office." He sucked air again. "I'm different."

"Office," she sneered. "Valentine for President?"

Jake worked out the syllables in his head before he spoke them. "Legislature."

"You're an ass," Paula repeated. "A user."

She turned to go.

"Ass," she said again, heading to her car.

Jake watched her go, then looked at his shoes.

On her favorite bench, Alice blinked and swallowed hard.

13.

Ruby came home weak. Aunt Lela bought her new clothes, smaller than before, but Ruby rarely went out. She let her hair go frizzy. Uncle George diligently bought new books for her to read. School was too taxing, but they arranged for a teacher to come to the house twice a week. Ruby ate little at first. "Please, Ruby, eat," Aunt Lela said. But she had no appetite. "If you don't eat, you won't get stronger." Ruby made an attempt. At each meal, she ate a bit more than she really wanted. "Oh, Ruby, please eat," Aunt Lela said anyway. Gradually Ruby got a bit stronger. But her days were still short. She would rise arduously, move slowly. She would need a nap at midday. She would retire early.

She was standing at the corner of Uncle George's desk, licking an envelope, when the desk phone rang and startled her. Since the illness, a jolt like that always sent an ache in a kind of wave through her body. She needed to sit down. She lowered herself into Uncle George's desk chair.

"Ruby, can you answer it, honey?" Aunt Lela called from the kitchen. "I am up to my elbows in grease!"

"Hello."

"Mrs. Thomas?"

"No, Mrs. Thomas is not available at this moment. This is Ruby."

There was a silence.

"May I help you? My Aunt Lela might be able to come to the phone in a minute."

"Ruby Tillmore?"

"Yes. Who is this?"

"Heavens. Ruby Tillmore."

"Who is this?"

"My name is Margaret Pierce. Is Mr. George Thomas available to talk?"

"Ugh, what a mess!" Aunt Lela was wringing her hands with a towel as she walked. "I'll take it, Ruby."

Ruby handed her the phone.

"Hello, this is Lela Thomas."

"Mrs. Thomas, my name is Margaret Pierce. Is your husband there? I should really speak with him, as the one who signed our forms here."

"He's running errands for me in town," Lela said. "What forms? Where are you calling from?"

"I am the doctor in charge at Clement Finnegan Institution."

"Clement Finnegan?"

"Finnegan!" Ruby cried, jumping up. "Maddie!"

"I am not really supposed to be calling——"

"What's wrong with Maddie!" Ruby demanded.

Lela pursed her lips at the outburst, trying to keep her attention on the telephone. "Is there — something wrong — with Maddie?" she stuttered.

"I want you to understand," Pierce continued, "that when your husband assigned your niece into our care, he agreed in writing to the severance of all rights."

"Yes, I understand."

"But I felt I had to contact you because——"

"Because?"

"Your niece is going to have a baby."

"A — baby."

Ruby's knees felt soft. "A baby."

Lela's face was stone. "When?"

"Any day. Maddie is healthy. She is going to be fine. I felt I should call you because of Ruby's letters."

"Ruby's letters?"

"She seems — It seems there's — a tie there."

"What about my letters?" Ruby wanted to know.

"Officially, we're supposed to send the baby to Sangamon. The orphanage. But I thought you——"

"What about my letters," Ruby said.

"I didn't know if you would want to consider taking the baby."

"Taking it," Lela echoed. Her voice sounded hollow. Ruby held out her hand. "Let me talk to her. Please." Aunt Lela turned away. "I have to talk with my husband about this."

"Of course."

"Give me the phone," Ruby said.

"Do you want me to give you the phone number here? Perhaps your husband will want to call me."

"Yes, yes," Lela stammered. "Let me — I'll need to write it down—"

She turned back toward the desk. Ruby pulled the phone from her hand.

"What happened to Maddie?"

"Ruby, let me talk with your aunt, please."

"Tell me."

"She's going to have a baby. Soon. She's going to be fine."

"What about the baby."

"The baby will be fine."

"Will it come here?"

Silence.

"Will it?"

"I don't know."

"I will take the baby."

"Ruby," Lela interjected. "You can't."

"You can't," Pierce said sadly. "Your letters. You seem so—"

"I can."

"You've had tuberculosis," Pierce explained. "I can't let a baby go to — that kind of situation. It would have to be — your uncle and aunt."

Ruby stood silent, her face a grim rock.

"Give me the phone," Lela said.

Ruby held it out to her and sat back down.

Uncle George returned within the hour, and he could hear their voices before he got to the door.

"An orphanage!" Ruby was shrieking.

"I don't know; we have to talk," Lela replied, each word scraping.

"You would do it! You would let Maddie's baby go!" Ruby's face was blotchy with tears.

"It is not a simple thing," Lela answered.

The door opened. "George! Thank the Lord."

The story spilled out. George sat, stunned at first. But then he set his jaw.

"It is not practical," he said squarely, "for us to have a baby here."

"I'll take care of it!"

"Ruby, it is not practical——"

"It's a baby," she shot back, savagely.

"We were willing to take you," Lela cut in.

"Thank you!" Ruby gasped with rage.

"But a baby!" Lela persisted.

George raised one hand. "It was one thing to take you in, Ruby——"

"Trade me then," she interrupted. "Take Maddie's baby. Let me go. I'll find another place."

"Ruby, you're too weak to get through a day. You can't go — and you can't care for a baby."

"Look at all this!" Ruby shouted. "Look at this big house! Look at this money! You could do it! You could if you wanted!" She was sobbing now, and she was exhausted. She collapsed on the couch. Lela looked at George, whose face said nothing, and she sat next to Ruby tentatively. She put an arm around her shoulders.

"Ruby, dear, you don't know where this baby came from. It could be a——"

Ruby pulled away from her and stood, then had to steady herself again on the arm of the couch. "A what? A monster?" Her eyes dug into Lela, then George. "That what you think?"

There was quiet, except for Ruby's hard breathing.

"Some folk can be monsters even when you know where they came from."

Lela's mouth opened. "Ruby!"

"Give me bus fare," Ruby said, staring straight at George. "Bus fare back to Leland."

"Ruby, you can't."

"Is it too much money for you? Can't afford it? Let's sell the drapes. Sell the furniture!"

"Ruby!" Lela yelped. "You're hysterical."

"I'm human. You wouldn't know."

George flinched. "That is not fair, Ruby."

"Give me money for the bus," Ruby said evenly.

George crumpled. "Let's talk about it in the morning."

"Give me the money, or I'll steal it from you. Or I'll steal it from your neighbors. I'll get it somehow." Against the glare of a window in the background, her fuzzy hair flared like a crown of sparks. "You may as well give it to me. I'm going, and you can help me or not."

A sheet of silence settled over the room. Ruby could hear her heartbeat in her ears. George's eyes swung from place to place, not finding anything to look at. Pearls of perspiration glistened over his eyebrows. Lela's face was a frozen mask, alarm and pain. Finally George's gaze settled on Lela.

"All right," George said hoarsely.

Lela turned to Ruby. "I'll go with you."

"No."

You don't want the baby. You'll get there and let them give it away.

"It's not safe for you to travel so——"

"No. I'll be fine."

14.

Jake is late again. The house is so silent. Alice makes tea and sits in the dusk. In her kitchen, but she is still back on her favorite bench.

I heard him say it. "I'm different now. I'm a family man."

I knew what he was like, before. That woman was from before.

I took the chance. I thought about it. I thought it through. I didn't fool myself. I didn't rush. I didn't push. Did I?

He held her off. *That bitch.* He's different now.

Women from back then will still be around. They'll come around. He can't help that. He can only tell them no.

He did. I heard him. He stood his ground. He's mine.

"You wait awhile to find a husband." Her mother's face is so open, her knitting needles still and silent. She sighs so deeply, a sigh of longing for her young daughter. *"A good man will be easier to enjoy."*

I do, Mommy. I do enjoy him. He's wonderful. He sparkles. Life is so good with Jake.

"Goddammit, Martha, come here! I oughta walk outa here and never come back."

Jake didn't do anything wrong to me. To us. He stood up for us. He's not like Daddy.

I'll ask him about the woman in the park. I'll ask him to tell me all about it. Who she is. When it happened.

"I've had plenty of women. I don't need this aggravation."

No. Jake will be so hurt. So embarrassed. He loves me so much. Look how he put that woman off. I don't want to know about her. If I have to know about her, do I have to know about all the others? The ones before me?

"The hell I did."

"I'm not a fool, Harv."

"You're with me. What's that make ya?"

No. We'll go forward. Not backward. Only forward. We're already going forward. We've been going forward. Nothing has changed. Except Jake. He changed. He said so.

"I'll find me a good woman, goddammit."

I'm not you, Mommy. I'm not becoming you. I won't go through what you went through with Daddy. Because Jake's not Daddy. He's not like that. He's different. We're different.

"Stop it, I said."

"Goddammit, come on."

That soft laugh. Or a chuckle? "Oh." Her mother's voice, soft and low. "Oh."

In the twilight, the surface of the tea is rippling. Two of Alice's tears have fallen into the cup. She backs her head away and wipes her face with the back of her hand.

"I'm a family man. I'm going to be a father."

I love him. We're in love. It's real. It's stronger than — anything before. We're stronger.

"I'm different."

He's different, Mommy.

Oh, Jake. Please be.

The tea is cold.

I don't think that will be my favorite bench anymore.

The kitchen door rattles. Alice takes a napkin to her face.

"I'm late! I know!" Jake crows. "But wait till you hear! Barnes! I got the Barnes account!"

He stomps happily to her, slips a hand behind her head and kisses her hair. "Barnes is big," he says in a mock whisper.

Oh Jake. So beautiful. Are you mine?

"How can you read in the dark?" He reaches for the light switch and flicks it. "Barnes! What can I *buy* you? This is big!"

Those high cheekbones. Those bright eyes. Please be mine.

Jake pulls out the other kitchen chair and plops down with a huge smile. Laughter erupts from him, and he shakes his head. "Barnes! Oh, Alice!"

Oh Jake. I know you're mine. You must be mine.

* * *

Ruby had never seen Aunt Lela cry, but her eyes were wet. She had packed a basket with food, a jar of juice, and a jar of water. And a small suitcase with clothing and essentials. She kissed Ruby on the hair, and Uncle George drove her to the bus station.

He bought her ticket, round trip, and gave her a man's wallet with more money than she had ever actually seen. He wanted her to have enough for cab fare, if necessary, from Leland proper out to Finnegan and back, and enough for meals and lodging. She would arrive on the wrong end of Leland to get to darktown safely. She would need a place close to the bus station.

Part of the money, he said, she should keep in her clothes. His face was rigid as she climbed onto the bus.

She sat in the back. Nobody bothered her. It was a stuffy tube. It jostled and rattled. It hissed to a stop, roared to a start. It jostled and rattled again. Ruby slept and woke, ate and drank, slept and woke.

By Leland, at dusk, she had been achily, irritably awake for a long time. She struggled up the aisle of the bus with her two pieces. The bus driver took the suitcase and lowered it to the ground after her. The door slapped shut behind her. The bus station hunched to one side, chipped paint and gray window panes. It had been located a frustrating distance from the square, as if someone had wanted to hide the town from people passing through — or had regarded bus travel as somehow beneath Leland's dignity. But someone years before had shrewdly erected a hotel near the bus station — a tiny hotel, by now decayed into a gray, paint-chipped twin of the bus station. Ruby lugged her burdens there.

A stout white woman with a faint brown mustache checked her in.

"You're traveling alone?" she inquired with a skeptical look. "Yes," Ruby answered wearily.

"You seem young to be traveling alone."

Ruby was too exhausted for dialogue. "Can I stay here? I have money."

"Well," the woman responded uneasily, "how long will you be staying?"

"Just tonight," Ruby said. "I think."

The woman looked around, as if to assure herself the lobby was empty. "Well, yes, we have a room for you." She took Ruby's name and money. "Follow me." They walked through the kitchen toward the back of the building, into a dim, narrow hall, then through a faded door smudged with decades of fingerprints. There was a small cubicle with a narrow bed, a cracked sink, a dead fly.

The woman left her, closing the door behind her. Ruby had never stayed in a hotel. This was not exactly how she had imagined it. But she was too tired to carry the thought. She took off the limp clothes of the long journey, splashed the dead fly down the drain, took a tattered rag that hung on a peg and washed her face.

To Ruby, Aunt Lela's gift was elegant, a nightgown, long and satiny, bestowed only a week before. Ruby pulled the covers up to her chin, then switched to her side, pulled up her knees, and began to cry. A grinding fatigue was wringing her. For so long now she had closed, closed, closed the doors. Closed the door on her mother. Closed the door on the dirt field, on Henry, on Tobias. She had kept Uncle George and Aunt Lela outside the door. She had even kept Maddie out, only cracking it a bit, on

Friday nights — but then quickly retreating again. Now here she was, back in Leland, back home but far from home. Back in her town, but all alone. The tears burned her eyes. A door in her heart flung open. She wanted her mother. Another door, and another door. She longed for Henry, Tobias, her girlfriends. She longed for the dirt field and baseball. The doors kept banging open. She even wanted Uncle George and Aunt Lela. Ruby sobbed into the thin pillow.

"Mama," she whimpered. "Mama."

But finally the anguish wrung itself out. She began to catch her breath. She wiped her face. She closed a door. She closed another. She closed them all.

She slept hard.

She woke feeling tight, like a string. She was surprised by the daylight. It had been morning for some time. She pulled her hair back tight. The morning bus to Finnegan was long gone. Ruby asked the woman in the office to call a taxi.

The driver of the cab had the same look on his face as the hotel clerk.

"That's a long way," he huffed. "Finnegan."

"How much will it cost?" Ruby asked curtly.

He gave her the figure.

"I got that."

He did not move.

"I'll pay you now, if that's what you want."

He rolled his tongue into his cheek. "Yeah."

She paid him. He hoisted her bags into the cab. She let herself in and closed the door.

"Finnegan, huh?" the driver said into the rear-view mirror once they were out on the road.

Ruby said nothing.

"Got family out there?"

Ruby looked out the window.

"I said, you got someone at Finnegan?"

Ruby looked at his eyes in the mirror. "My sister."

"She crazy?"

"She got hit on the head."

"Oh." He drummed his fingers on the steering wheel. "How she get hit on the head? Accident?"

Ruby fingered the wallet George had given her. She wedged it open and calculated how much money was left.

"She get in a fight?"

"With a baseball."

"What?"

"She got hit on the head with a baseball."

The driver looked numbly into the mirror. Then he murmured unhappily — "Baseball, damn" — and drove the rest of the way in silence.

Only rarely did a black person arrive as a patient at Finnegan, and almost never as a visitor. Everett could not recall ever seeing a black person get out of a taxicab in front of the venerable white columns. But now he had. He had just brought two fat chairs, newly re-upholstered over in Leland, into the front parlor, and he was returning to move the truck around back. The wheels of the taxi crunched over the gravel as it rolled away. Ruby looked small.

"Whatcha need?" Everett asked.

"I'm here to see a doctor. Margaret, or Martha, I'm not sure. But Pierce."

"Margaret Pierce. Sure." Everett started to hold the door, then decided to help her with her bags instead. But he stopped just at the door and turned to her.

"You — are you—?"

"My sister is here. Maddie Tillmore."

Everett's eyes opened wide. "Did Pierce write to you or something?"

"She called my aunt and uncle. Why?"

Everett pressed his tongue against his upper lip. "Let me — oh boy." He took in a sharp breath. "Let's do Pierce a favor, and take you in around the back."

He carried the bags. Ruby followed him. They traipsed around half the exterior of the building and ended up at the disorganized back entrance, with vehicles and a garage door and a makeshift loading dock. Everett led Ruby through a door and into a kitchen. He set her bags on the floor.

"You can sit right there," he said, gesturing toward the table. "You wait right here, and I'll bring Pierce — Dr. Pierce."

Ruby sat down. Everett hurried out. It did not seem like long before she heard two sets of footsteps thunking rapidly toward the kitchen. Pierce, short and sturdy, appeared in the doorway, Everett over her shoulder. The doctor's eyes were round.

"Heavens," she rasped, as if speaking through a squeezebox. "Are you Ruby?"

"Yes, are you——?"

"Margaret Pierce." She looked at Ruby in blank astonishment, then stepped forward to shake her hand. Ruby was startled to be offered a white woman's hand. Slowly, she took it.

Pierce pulled another chair back from the table and sat down.

Ruby eyed her quizzically. "You don't sound like the doctor on the telephone."

Pierce was looking around almost frantically. "Heavens. Ruby. What? Oh — I have laryngitis. Where's that ash tray?"

Everett stepped in from the doorway and lifted a saucer out of the sink. "Here."

Everett had never seen Pierce with a cigarette. He watched in silent surprise as she withdrew a small flat metal box from her omnipresent black bag. She opened it and fumbled getting a cigarette into her mouth. Then she got the box closed and back in the bag, but she couldn't find matches.

"Damn," she croaked.

Everett snapped out of it and stepped forward again, this time with a match.

"Where's Maddie?" Ruby asked.

"She's here," Pierce answered, dragging a smoke. "She's fine. But Ruby, what are you doing here?"

"I came to take the baby."

"Do your uncle and aunt know you're here?"

"They gave me the money for the trip."

"They — heavens." She sucked on the cigarette.

"I made them do it. I told them I'd steal it."

"Ruby, I wish you had called me."

Ruby gave her a questioning look. "I thought my uncle did. He said he would."

Pierce propped her elbow on the table and rubbed her forehead. "I was sick at home yesterday — with this." She waved derisively at her own throat. "I haven't even caught up to my messages."

"I want to see Maddie."

"Ruby, I would have told you not to come here."

"Why? My aunt and uncle said I could. They gave me money."

"Because it's against the rules, that's why. Your uncle signed Maddie over to us, and that means he doesn't have any rights to her baby."

"I'm her sister. I'm family."

"You're under-age, Ruby."

"I'm eighteen!"

Pierce looked hard at her.

"Maddie and me was twins." Everett watched Ruby blinking fast, signaling the lie.

Pierce moaned with frustration. "I can't let you take a baby. And you're sick. Look at you. You're gray. You're even weaker than you said in your letters."

Ruby's eyes flashed. "Why did you read my letters? They wasn't yours."

"It's my job. When mail comes for patients, I have to open it. It's to protect the patients."

Ruby's eyes were hot.

"But it's against the law for me to throw out anybody's mail. So I still have every one of your letters in my files. I'll give them back to you if you want."

Ruby shifted in her chair. "I want to see Maddie."

Pierce suddenly twisted around toward the doorway, as if she had not even noticed Everett standing there. "Would you excuse us?" she rasped. "Wait. No, stay. I think I may need you."

Everett lazily fished a cigarette out of his pocket. He lit it and leaned on the door frame.

"Ruby." Pierce leaned in and touched her hand, but she pulled it away. "Ruby, I will get in serious trouble if the chairman of the trustees learns that you came here. I could lose my job. I wasn't supposed to contact you or your family. I only did it be-cause — because of your letters."

"What?"

"You seemed, in your letters, like — you loved her so much. And like your aunt and uncle might — they might be able to——"

"You saw they had money."

"Well, yes."

Ruby sat lower in the chair. "That don't matter. They won't take a baby."

"Ruby. Heavens. What did you think you were going to do?"

"I think we got other family."

"Think? Not here in Leland?"

Ruby winced a little at the thought of her cousin Shirley in the one-room shack. "No. My mother had a brother. He went to prison, but he was married, I think. I could ask his wife."

"Where is she?"

Everett shifted his weight and followed the waves of tension in Ruby's face.

"Chicago, I think."

"You think. Ruby! Heavens."

"What's their name?" Everett cut in. "You could call them."

"I don't know."

Pierce squinted through the smoke.

"My Uncle George might know," Ruby offered faintly.

"All right," Pierce said, plunging the butt into the saucer. "I'll call him and see. Now I need to get you out of here without Dr. Shaw seeing you."

"I want to see Maddie."

"Yes, I know. In a minute. Where are you staying?"

"Last night, in the hotel by the bus stop."

Pierce looked up at Everett and opened her mouth to speak, but Ruby interrupted.

"I can't keep staying there. I don't have enough money."

Pierce sat back heavily in the chair. Her hands were on the table; her fingers tapped the surface.

Everett chuckled. "Take her home, Mama."

Pierce shot a withering glance at him — then looked abruptly at Ruby and softened. "I'm sorry, Ruby, but I can't bring you to my house. My neighbors." She glared at Everett again. "You know that, Everett. God, it would be trouble."

He seemed unfazed. He shifted his weight again, leaned against the doorpost, and blew smoke. "The mission?"

Ruby jerked to attention. "The mission. In Leland. I could. I could go there. I know the lady."

"Fine," Pierce said, waving a hand at Everett. "You drive her."

"Okay," Everett said, shrugging to straighten himself up.

"No, I want to see Maddie."

"Yes, heavens," Pierce said. "After you see Maddie." She looked nervously at her wristwatch and stood up. "I've got to get back. You walk her around back to the infirmary. Go ahead of her and make sure nobody's in those windows." She stepped toward the hallway; Everett came in to make room for her.

"Infirmary?" Ruby asked, also standing. "What's 'infirmary'?"

Everett picked up her bags. "It's like our little hospital here," he said.

Ruby pushed back her chair and stumbled a bit standing up. "Hospital? Is Maddie sick?"

Pierce turned back in the doorway with a face of puzzlement. "No, Ruby," she said, as if she had been saying it all morning. "Maddie had her baby last night."

15.

Alice looked up from her desk, and her mouth fell open. "Ruby?"

Ruby set her bags down. Alice came running, and threw her arms around the girl. Ruby hugged back — and then shocked herself by exploding into tears.

"Oh, friend," Alice said, touching the back of her pale hand to Ruby's dark cheek. "You're safe now."

Ruby sobbed into Alice's blouse. Alice laid her hand on the fuzz of her unkempt hair.

"Please tell me what's happened."

She led Ruby to a pair of chairs. They sat down, and the story poured out. Deenah's death. Uncle George and Aunt Lela. The sanatorium. The call from Dr. Pierce.

"Oh, Lord," Alice whispered.

"It's a boy."

Ruby's heart was pounding.

"He's beautiful. He's — he's blond."

Alice's face didn't change.

"Blond, with big curls."

Ruby shifted in the chair. She looked hard at Alice. Driving here with Everett, she had imagined this moment, her mind dancing in difficult steps, grasping for the future. There was a long, thin silence as she gathered her courage.

"Can you take him?"

Alice's face pulled back. "Take him?"

"Take the baby. Be the parents. His parents."

Alice stared at her.

"He's beautiful," Ruby offered weakly.

"Oh, Ruby." Alice took a deep breath. "I'm sure he's a beautiful baby."

"Don't you and mister want no babies?"

Alice's mouth opened, then closed, then opened again. "Yes, we do. But—" She stood.

"Maddie's baby is a baby."

Silence fell again.

"No family to take him," Ruby said softly. "I could tell by the way she talked. The doctor, I mean. He's a problem for them. There's trouble there, at Finnegan, because Maddie had a baby. I don't know what they'll do to him."

Alice's eyes narrowed.

Ruby looked squarely at her. "He's my blood."

Alice took a few steps back and forth. Her arms were folded tight across her belly. "Oh, Ruby." Ruby watched Alice's fingers rhythmically clenching and unclenching, and she felt a ripple of nausea. Her brain snapped electrically, searching for help.

"You told me," Ruby finally blurted. Then she continued calmly. "You told me what Jesus did."

Alice stopped and looked at her.

"Helped people who couldn't help themselves."

Alice said nothing. She bit her lower lip, took another deep breath and let it out.

"Let's go have dinner at my house," she finally said. "We'll talk to Jake."

Ruby looked at her sharply. "Will it be all right?"

Alice was puzzled.

"Eating together? With me?"

Alice glanced at the window. "Yes, Ruby. You can eat with us, of course."

* * *

He came through the door laughing, tossing his hat.

"What a day! Those Randover people are crazy!"

Alice came around the corner and slipped an arm around his middle. "We have a guest," she said quietly.

Her tone made Jake stop and look at her.

"Okay," he responded tentatively.

In the front room, Ruby stood politely.

"Jake, this is my friend Ruby Tillmore."

Jake couldn't suppress his surprise. But he only missed a beat, then recovered, extending his hand. "Well, hello there, young lady."

"Hello," Ruby said with a shy handshake, looking at his fingers as they wrapped around her hand. She suppressed a shudder of amazement, realizing that she had touched more white skin in the last two days than in her entire life.

"To what do we owe the honor?" Jake asked, looking from Ruby to Alice and back again.

"Ruby's going to have dinner with us," Alice said simply. "We have a little story to tell you."

"A little story?" he replied, slipping out of his coat.

"Well, maybe not so little."

Jake stood at the closet and turned to her with a sort of grin. "Could you at least tell me the topic now?"

Alice looked at Ruby and seemed to shrug a bit.

"It's possible that we're going to have a baby."

Jake's face flickered — from shock to joy, then to puzzlement. Looking at Ruby's brown face, he saw fear. And maybe something else.

* * *

Alice layered blankets on the couch for Ruby.

Soon, Jake and Alice lay on their backs, looking straight up into the darkness, speaking in low tones like parents hoping the child will sleep.

"Tomorrow I'll take her to her cousin's place, and see if she can stay there."

"Okay."

Silence.

"Jake?"

"Yeah."

"What are you thinking?"

"Just thinking." Silence. "It's a lot to think about."

"I know."

She touched his hand and slipped her fingers around three of his fingers.

"It's sudden, you know?"

"I know."

She squeezed.

"I'm sorry there's not more time," Alice said. "To decide."

"Yeah, me too."

Silence.

"Jake, I don't know if I can have a baby." The words scraped.

Jake frowned in the darkness. "Don't say that."

"I don't. It could be impossible. Something could be wrong."

"Nothing's wrong."

"We don't know that."

Silence.

Jake let out a long, slow breath. "Maybe we could go look at him."

"To, what?"

"To, I don't know, look at him."

Alice moved her hand from his fingers up to the crook of his elbow. "To see what color he is?"

"No."

"To make sure he's not too dark?"

"No, of course not."

"Then," and she waited. It was quiet again.

"What," Jake finally said.

"Are we saying we won't love him if he's not the right color? Not light enough?"

"Geez, Alice, no." But Jake twisted his torso for no obvious reason. "No."

She paused. "I think," and paused again, and then spoke even more softly than before. "I think a baby needs to be loved no matter what color he is."

"Of course."

Silence.

"You know what would happen," Jake finally said. "Honestly. Think about it. I know we want a baby, but honestly. This baby isn't one of us."

"He's not white," Alice replied evenly.

"He's not white!" Jake snapped, turning his face to her. "He's not white. It matters, Alice. You may be all liberal and full of compassion for coloreds, but your neighbors aren't."

"And you?"

"Oh come on." Jake dropped his head back onto the pillow.

"The Cleveland Indians have colored players now."

Jake turned sharply toward her. "You follow *baseball*?"

"No, I read about it in the *New Yorker*. The Dodgers hired Jackie Robinson. Everybody screamed. Then the Indians brought in two Negro players and won the pennant."

"Not this year."

"Jake, you said there are Negroes working at the factory."

"It's not the same, for heaven's sake. It's work. It's not a family."

"They're people, aren't they?"

"Oh come on. I know they're people. But colored people have colored children. White people have white children."

"No Negro family will take him, you know that," Alice said steadily. "And no white family will take him. Not around here. Except we could." Silence. "If we want to."

Jake stared into the inkiness. He breathed deeply. "This is pretty crazy, Alice."

"I know."

Silence again.

"Are you worried about running?"

"Running?"

"For the legislature. If you have a colored child."

Jake shifted awkwardly. "Well, it won't help."

Alice turned toward him and lifted herself on an elbow. "Is that really it? You can tell me if it is."

"What?"

"You're afraid you can't win if you have a colored child?"

"Of course not." Jake looked away. "I don't know."

Alice sat up. The sheet slid down as she raised her knees and wrapped her arms around them. She looked straight ahead into the darkness.

"I don't even know if I can run," Jake said. "I can't run if Jessup doesn't get his people behind me. I don't know what he'd say about — this." Jake's voice had the metallic edge of annoyance.

"So," Alice said, "it's really up to Gordon Jessup."

"No!"

"Whether we have the baby or not."

"No! God."

Alice lowered her head. "Jake, I love you. I don't want to push you. But there's no time. I'm sorry there's no time. They'll do something with the baby right away. We have to decide what we we're going to do. We have to know what we really believe."

"Believe?"

"If we believe people are people. If we believe it's wrong to make colored people keep to themselves, unless they're working for us."

"It's not just what we believe!" Jake cried. "It's everybody else."

Alice sat silent. Then she shivered and pulled the sheet up over her knees.

"Look at you, Jake. You're a leader." Her voice was steady. "You make people agree with you."

Jake sighed hard, as if he'd been holding his breath.

"I can see you running. I can see you winning. I can't see you being afraid."

Jake shifted again on his back. He reached out to slip his hand behind her calf.

"I have to sleep now," he said.

"Me too."

Jake lay still, then withdrew his hand and turned on his side, away from her. Alice looked at the line of his silhouette in the gloom. Fatigue fell heavy over her. She slid down under the covers and moved herself away.

* * *

Pierce turns onto her left side, doesn't like the way her shoulder feels, turns to her right, and doesn't like that either. Her stomach growls in the dark. She reaches for the lamp, pulls the chain, and scowls at the clock.

"Jesus."

She throws back the covers and pushes her legs over the edge of the bed, takes the pack from the nightstand and taps out a cigarette. She strikes a match, lights up, draws deep.

Jesus. A baby.

Shaw will have my head.

Where the hell will I ever find work?

She inhales again.

How far away will I have to go? God damn this.

She looks at the burning end, but doesn't see it. She sees the baby.

Shaw's right. Sangamon. The orphanage. That girl's not going to find family to take a baby like that. Blond mulatto.

But Ruby's letters drift through her head. Ruby's careful scrawl, page after page after page of it. And now, Ruby's face. Her face won't go away.

Pierce pulls hard on the cigarette, crushes it in the ashtray, pushes the smoke out through her nose. She pulls the chain and drops back onto the pillow.

Jesus. A baby.

* * *

Ruby settled onto the blankets, curled up, closed her eyes, let out all the air. She saw Maddie, sleeping in the infirmary bed, a silent angel, moon-shaped smudges of exhaustion under her eyes. The memory coils tight around Ruby's throat, pushing tears between her eyelids. She saw the baby, so odd, such bright brown skin, such strange ashen-yellow hair, such big, hopeful curls. Beautiful dark eyes, still learning to focus. Tiny, perfect fingers, still learning to feel.

Ruby's spine twinged. She wiggled to change position. Weariness crushed her, but her brain was sparking. She felt a line, like electricity, stretched from her heart all the way to Finnegan, to the baby, to the baby's heart. Her heart was thrumming, desperate to keep the power on, keep the line alive, the connection. Thoughts swirled like fog. *Keep the baby. My blood. Don't cut my family apart.* The fog thickened. The electric line hummed but dimmed. Thoughts thinned, and dissipated. Sleep slid over her.

* * *

A hammer was pinging in Jake's head, like machinery gone bad.

"*The Cleveland Indians have colored players now.*"

That's stupid, Alice. This isn't a baseball team. It's real life. And this isn't Cleveland. It's Leland.

"*If he's not the right color?*"

Jake's brain flashed black faces, brown faces, tan faces. Mr. Feagle's gleaming smile as he looked up from the conveyor. Johnson in the back. Farraday under the window. Mrs. Kinsey, shiny black with sweat. Patsy. Freddy. Thelma.

"*Not light enough?*"

It makes a difference, Alice. People care. Maybe it's not right, but they do. We're going to convince them otherwise? A brown-skinned baby is okay in a white neighborhood? In a white family?

"*It's really up to Gordon Jessup.*"

No. Taking the baby, no. It's not up to Jessup. But running — as the father of a mixed-race child? Yes. That's the real world, Alice. It's up to Gordon Jessup.

"*If we believe people are people.*"

No, damn it. It's not up to Jessup whether we believe it. Of course people are people. It's just the world, Alice. It's just how the world is.

"*Look at you, Jake. You're a leader.*"

Damn, Alice. All right. Skin color doesn't matter. Only in people's heads. Jessup can decide what he wants. But we have to decide what *we* want. If we want this baby.

"*You make people agree with you.*"

Damn, Alice. I agree with you.

"*I can't see you being afraid.*"

Jake twisted over onto his stomach, onto his elbows. His head dropped toward his pillow. In the murk, Jake stared at his pillowcase, a jangle of wrinkles in a kind of bowl where his skull had been. Opposite the pinging in his head, Alice's breathing was soft and steady at his side.

A baby. Boom! Just like that.

Jake lay perfectly still, willing the hammer to stop.

Hold the baby. Feed the baby. Change the diaper. Family man. Tomorrow!

He held his breath and felt his pulse in his temple with each ping of the hammer.

A new life, Jakey. All new. Family man!

A young woman drifted into his head, then another, and another, and more, all staring at him, wincing a little with each hammer blow, then glowering more and more deeply after each impact, as if he displeased them. Katherine Abbott smirked. Paula Ricard chortled. Jake tensed his stomach muscles.

It's not a bad thing. To have a good life – to be good. It's good.

The women's faces bobbed sarcastically in the mist. Their necks came into view, their collarbones, their cleavage. Jake's jaw was locked tight.

I'll be a good father.

Their eyebrows arched. Their chins came up. They licked their lower lips.

The possibility of the pleasure.

Their fingers came up, stroked their skin at the edge of their clothing.

The pull of the power.

Jake tried to steady his breathing. His face felt hot.

Things change. A baby will change everything. A baby will need a good father. A good person. A baby will help me.

The pinging began to subside, as if someone had put the machine on a cart and begun dragging it into the distance.

* * *

"I think you're right."

Alice opened her eyes in the dark. "What?"

Jake was lying on his back, but with his head up straight, the pillow tucked behind his head. "I think you're right."

"About what?"

"About loving him. I think you're right. It can't be about being the right color." He took his time. "I mean, this is 1950. It's not the Civil War anymore."

Silence.

"I couldn't go back into the factory and look Feagle in the eye."

"Feagle?"

"The Negro. And tell him I wouldn't love a baby because of its color? Too dark. Too light. It can't be right."

More silence.

"If Jessup backs me, and I run, and people complain, I'll just have to — I don't know, *charm* them."

Alice lay still. Jake exhaled again. It was quiet a long while.

"I don't think we can go look at him," he finally said.

"No?"

"I think if we're going at all, we have to say we're going to take him, and love him. Whatever color he is. Regardless."

They were quiet again, for a long time. When Alice opened her mouth, Jake could hear her silent tears.

"I know you thought we'd have a baby of our own."

Jake rolled onto one elbow to face her. In the blackness, he could catch the burnish of her wet cheeks.

"He *will* be our own," Jake said. "He'll be my son." He reached for her ear, and stroked its outer edge. "You'll be his mother." His fingers slipped down to caress her neck. "His beautiful mother."

Alice plunged into him, holding him tight with her free arm. Her face pressed into his chest, her mouth stretched tight against her sobs. He pulled her even closer, his hand in the middle of her back. He could feel her tears burn hot, then turn cold on his skin.

"I love you," she mumbled.

When he finally felt her relax, he eased his grip. "I'm sorry," he said.

She backed her face away and looked at him. "What?"

He grunted and let her go. "I can't do this on one elbow anymore."

She sputtered and stifled a laugh. He began to giggle.

"Shh!" Alice hissed, but they were both erupting and wheezing. Her laughter was a series of little chokes at the back of her throat. Jake was laughing in a rhythmic high-pitched staccato.

"Quiet!" he was finally able to gasp.

"Stop it!" she rasped.

By the time their bodies finally stopped convulsing, they were holding each other tight again. They breathed hard, pressed into each other's bodies. The air was thick with their after-laughter, but the energy of their joy was throbbing away, bouncing softly, slowly, into the black invisible. Their breathing was heavy, as their bodies recovered, and their lungs were out of sync. Then they were lying on their backs again, his arm around the back of her head, her arm at an angle, with her hand on his thigh.

"I bet," he said.

Her fingers pressed a bit into his flesh. "What?"

"I bet that girl I saw, at Finnegan," and his teeth clamped as he thought back to that day.

"What girl?"

"That Negro girl, the one I saw, sleeping. At Finnegan."

"What?"

Jake's face turned, suddenly changed, toward Alice.

"He could be beautiful. The baby. I mean, really beautiful."

Alice lay still.

"That girl was beautiful."

Alice lay on her back, staring at the ceiling she couldn't see.

"I don't know how it couldn't be," Jake said.

"What do you mean?"

"That must be Ruby's sister," he said, his voice fuzzy with wonder. "She's the only black woman I've seen in the place."

"You've gone back?"

"Pretty big account."

Alice lay silent.

"You know those places," Jake said, with the casual tone of pondering. "Crazy people, sure, but not many black crazy people."

Alice frowned in the dark. "What?"

Jake arched an eyebrow, even though there was no one to see it.

"You don't find many black crazy people. Those places are for white crazy people. They let black crazy people die."

16.

Jake slipped out to head to work.

Ruby never stirred. The long days of anxiety, coiled tight, finally had no choice but to unravel, and she slept deeply. Only the sharp, sweet smell of bacon, and its sizzling, poked her awake.

"Oh!" she said, sitting up. "I'm sorry."

Alice turned from the stove, smiling. "Good morning, Ruby. Sorry about what?"

"I slept so long."

"I'm glad you did. You needed to rest."

Ruby rubbed a sticky eye.

"Get cleaned up and then we'll eat."

Ruby rose unsteadily. "Thank you."

At breakfast, Ruby took small bites, looking mostly at her plate.

"Jake will call Finnegan today, about the baby," Alice said quietly.

Ruby looked up with wide eyes.

"You'll take him?"

"We'll ask if they'll talk with us about it."

Ruby's eyes darkened.

"We want to. We want to take him."

Ruby's expression didn't change. "What does that mean?"

"It's not our decision alone. He's not our baby."

"He's Maddie's baby!"

"I know, but——"

"They can't give him away. Put him in an orphanage. He doesn't belong to them." Ruby's voice was tight and thin.

"I know, Ruby," Alice answered softly.

"If Maddie gets well," Ruby said, then turned her face aside. Her eyes swelled red with tears.

Alice reached across the table and laid her hand over Ruby's. Ruby's grip on the fork relaxed. The fork clanged on the plate.

"I don't know about Maddie," Alice said, even more quietly.

"She never," Ruby gurgled, a fat tear rolling onto her cheek. "Never gonna get well." She pulled her hand away and covered her face.

Alice swallowed the lump in her throat. "Ruby, we'll do everything we can to get the baby." Ruby didn't look up from her silent sobbing. "Jake is good at talking. He's the best. He'll try to talk them into giving us the baby. I just can't," and her voice trailed off. Ruby looked up at her, her eyeballs spidery-red. "I can't guarantee anything. We don't have control of this."

"I should," Ruby said sharply. "I'm her sister."

"I know," Alice replied, with a dip of her head. "But you're sixteen."

"I'm almost seventeen. Next month I'm seventeen. Is it because I'm colored? And the baby is blond?"

"No, no," Alice murmured. "It's just — legalities."

Ruby's face held steady with anger, then went slack. She looked down at her plate.

"Thank you for breakfast," she said gently.

"You're welcome, of course," Alice said.

"And for everything."

Alice looked steadily at her. Then, suddenly, words popped out. "Oh! Ruby!" She pushed her chair back, jumped up from the table, and dashed away into her bedroom. "I have something for you!" She came back with a little box, wrapped in red paper.

She held it out to Ruby, but Ruby just looked at it in her extended hand. "For me?" she asked, her face a jumble of confusion.

"Open it!" Alice insisted.

Ruby took the box and turned it over, inspecting it. Her fingers went to the edge of the paper.

"Just tear it open," Alice said.

When Ruby took out the brass goose, her eyes brightened. "A goose!" She held it close to her face, then looked past it at Alice and smiled. "The fox and the corn," she said.

"You remembered!" Alice cheered.

"Oh, Alice!" Ruby exclaimed, setting the goose on the table and eyeing it like a treasure. "Of course I remember." She looked up at Alice. "The day I met you."

"That was a very good day."

Ruby sniffed and looked back at the goose.

Alice pointed to a box of tissues. "Blow your nose and help me with the dishes. Then we'll go to your cousin's."

Ruby stood, reached for the goose, and slipped it back into its box. She lowered her head and grinned sheepishly. "I'm so embarrassed."

Alice turned from the sink. "Why?"

"I said I'd kill that goose and eat it!"

Alice wrinkled her nose and began laughing, and then neither of them could stop.

* * *

"I don't think I've ever been in this neighborhood."

The LaSalle crawled through darktown.

"Turn here," Alice said as they approached Polk. She pointed at a tan shack. "That one."

Jake guided the car to a stop along the indistinct border between street and front yard. "That roof doesn't look too good," he said, killing the engine.

"You don't have to go with me."

"I think it would be better." Jake opened his door.

"I dropped Ruby here by myself on Saturday!"

"You dropped her off. That's not the same as going to the door."

"Ruby insisted I just drop her off."

"I'm not saying you aren't a big girl," Jake countered. He looked at her squarely. "Let's go."

As they approached, Alice was glad Jake was there. Her stomach tightened as she pictured the sullen, partially hidden woman she had talked with last winter.

Jake knocked on the front door, a little too solidly for Alice's taste. Then there was the clack of a bolt, and the door squeaked open.

"Hello, we're the Valentines, friends of Ruby's. I dropped her here on Saturday."

The door swung wide to reveal a narrow black woman with a red bandanna on her head. "Yes," she answered, without expression, then called over her shoulder. "Ruby! You got visitors."

"Oh, lordy," Ruby said as she came hurrying from the kitchen, wiping her hands on a rag, touching her hand to a head of hair pulled back tight and straight. "Hello! Shirley, these are my friends, Alice and Jake."

Shirley looked at them.

"Shirley is my cousin. She's let me stay here for a while."

Shirley stood still, against the wall, close to the door. Ruby gestured into the stuffy living room, with a threadbare green couch and an overstuffed orange chair. "Do you," she began, then wondered whether to go on. "Do you want to come in?"

"Thank you," Alice said, taking a step inside, "but we really didn't come to visit. Jake talked to Dr. Pierce at Finnegan, and she's willing to talk with us about taking the baby."

Ruby's eyebrows jumped. "Oh! That's good!"

"I think it would be better," Jake said, "if you came with us, Ruby."

Ruby's mouth opened, but for a second no sound came out. "All right!" she blurted. "I'll get my sweater." She hurried out of the room.

Alice turned to Shirley. Shirley was still just looking at them. "I'm sorry to intrude like this," Alice said.

"No, it's fine," Shirley replied. "It's good you here. I want to say a word to you."

Jake and Alice waited. Alice's jaw clenched.

"I was wrong," Shirley finally went on. "You a friend." She nodded gravely. "You a real friend."

Alice felt her face grow warm. "I — Thank you, Shirley. We — I am very fond of Ruby."

"Here I am," Ruby announced. She touched Shirley's hand as she passed. "Do we know when we'll be back?"

Jake turned back from the door. "We don't know a thing about anything," he said with a wry smile. "We're just going to have an adventure."

* * *

Ruby sat in the back seat. "So big," she murmured. "This car."

Alice twisted in the passenger seat to look at her. "You've ridden in this car before. "Twice before."

"I think it's getting bigger," Ruby said.

Alice chortled and faced the front. The LaSalle glided out of darktown, away from the dirt yards and scrawny shrubs and dead trees. Ruby watched the dirt field come and go. She could see the children clamoring for a chance to try the bat. She could see Maddie swinging like lightning, she could hear what must follow, the lightning-crack of the ball, she could follow the blur of Maddie's body ripping through the summer air to make base. Then, as the LaSalle kept gliding, there were leaves on the trees, the final glory before the autumn turning, and painted houses, and the proper lines and borders of what white folk called ordinary. And then the LaSalle pulled out onto the road to Finnegan.

It was quiet awhile before Ruby spoke again.

"You been kind to me, and I appreciate it."

"Don't worry about it, Ruby," Jake replied.

"But I need to ask you about something else. I'm gonna need work. I cleaned white folks' houses, but it ain't enough. I need regular work."

"Ruby, you have to go to school," Alice said.

"I could, but——" She bit her lip. "I told Dr. Pierce I'm eighteen."

"Eighteen!"

"I said Maddie and me was twins."

Jake looked sharply over his shoulder for a quick moment. "Did she believe that?"

"School here ain't much," Ruby continued. "The Negro school in Leland ain't really school."

"No?"

"In Pittsburgh, they had real school for colored."

The tires thumped along the road.

"Shirley has problems. She can't feed me, keep me, forever. I think I could work at Finnegan."

"At Finnegan!" Alice echoed.

"I seen colored people there, cleaning. Carrying food. Working in the yard. I could work. I'd work hard."

Alice turned around again. "And you could be close to Maddie."

"Yes," Ruby said quietly.

Alice looked at Jake. "Do you think we could ask about it today?"

"Alice, I don't know." His fingers flexed on the steering wheel. "We have a complicated situation on our hands as it is."

"I don't think this is a complication," Alice replied. "People apply for work all the time. We could just ask about it."

"I don't want trouble," Ruby said earnestly, from the back seat.

"It's not trouble," Alice insisted, still looking at Jake.

Jake glanced at her, his lips tight.

The LaSalle grumbled over a rough patch in the road.

"We'll see," he finally sighed.

17.

Erma greeted them at the door.

"Jake, welcome back," she said with a troubled smile. "Mrs. Valentine?"

"Alice," Alice said. "And you've met Ruby, I believe."

"Yes, I don't know if Dr. Pierce is expecting to meet with——"

"I think it will be fine, Erma," Jake interrupted, taking her gently by the arm and leaning his smile a bit toward her face.

"Yes, sir," she blushed. "Right this way."

Pierce's face was none too relaxed when they walked in, and when she saw Ruby, she hardened more.

"Dr. Pierce, thank you for seeing us," Jake began, extending his hand.

She shook it without gusto. Nobody sat down.

He made introductions.

"Yes, I know Ruby," Pierce said in her sandpaper voice. "I don't believe she should be present for this conversation."

Jake smiled. "Dr. Pierce, you know I value our relationship," he replied, his eyes gleaming. "I appreciate you as a customer, certainly, and I admire the work you're doing here at Finnegan."

"Yes, so?"

"I felt I needed sound advice about this situation, so I spoke to an attorney in town."

"Oh God," Pierce groaned. "We agreed you wouldn't speak about this to——"

Jake raised his palms reassuringly. "No names, no places, no specifics. Just the situation. I wanted to confirm."

"And?"

"Ruby is the baby's next of kin."

"She's under-age, Jake." Pierce's voice was sharp.

"She's eighteen."

Pierce looked at him incredulously.

"I've confirmed that too," he stated.

Pierce sighed heavily. "Let's sit down."

Alice glanced at Ruby's worried face. They sat. Alice gave Ruby a careful look, and raised her fingers off her lap just a bit, to signal the girl: *Just wait.*

"Dr. Pierce, I'd like to help you," Jake said. "You can't be having an easy time of it, caring for a baby here."

"God," Pierce groaned again. "Two of our nurses are handling it. It's impossible. But——" She looked from Jake to Alice to Ruby, and back at Jake. "Shaw, the chairman, pushed me to send him to Sangamon. The orphanage. But since Ruby showed up, the first day, I've — I guess I've stalled." The room was quiet. Pierce looked at her hands. "That place is so awful."

"Dr. Pierce," Jake said softly, "I appreciate your heart. None of us want the baby to go to the orphanage. But you have a serious public relations problem. Forgive me for being so direct, but one of your patients got pregnant, and nobody knows who did it. I'm sure you're concerned about losing your funding."

"If the baby goes to Sangamon," Pierce said wearily, "this problem disappears."

"No one there cares. They have no incentive to keep the story quiet. But let Ruby sign the baby over to Alice and me, we'll adopt him, and — well, obviously, none of us will want this little guy to grow up saddled with such a history. We adopted him — from an agency in Pittsburgh. End of story."

The air hung heavy and silent. Pierce had one hand to her head, her fingers scratching at her hairline. Finally she sat back heavily. She looked hard at Alice.

"I take it you agree with this?"

"I do, Dr. Pierce," Alice answered steadily. "I believe in God, and I believe this is God's will."

Pierce cocked her head quizzically. "Don't you want to see the baby before you decide this?"

Jake and Alice looked at each other, and replied in unison. "No."

Pierce shook her head. "Shaw will kill me if he finds out. But God, Sangamon. It's terrible. To send a child there, when a family is willing to take him—" She looked at nothing and shook her head again. "And you're right. This story getting out would be a disaster."

Jake raised his index finger, offering a new thought. "We could take the baby today, on an unofficial basis, of course."

Alice's eyes opened wide. "Yes!" she whispered.

"Like when you let your child spend the night at a friend's house," Jake continued. "Just until the paperwork is finished."

Pierce's face hesitated, then changed. It settled into a certain resolve. She stood.

"I'll send you home with everything we've gathered for him, to get you started."

She allowed herself a grim laugh. "The nurses went into some kind of frenzy, bringing things from their friends and relatives. Telling everyone his parents were visiting and had an accident, and he would only be with us a few days. Clothes, diapers, a baby bed."

Jake pointedly stayed in his chair, and crossed his legs. "There's one other detail I'd like to bring up with you," he said.

Pierce did not sit down.

"Ruby would like to come to work for you here."

Pierce turned to Ruby. "You need to be in school."

Ruby looked squarely at her.

"She finished school in Pittsburgh," Jake inserted.

Pierce's eyes half-closed with exhaustion. "You're not eighteen."

"Ma'am, I seen colored folks working here," Ruby said in a soft tone. "I'd work hard for you. Mopping. I can mop. I can clean. My mama cleaned white people's houses, and then I took over her business."

The doctor leaned against her desk. "I'd have to put you on overnight. I can't have people seeing you working here during school hours."

"Overnight's good," Ruby said. "I can do it."

Pierce didn't move. "All right. In maintenance."

Ruby glanced at Alice and stifled a smile.

"You check in Monday at 10 p.m. with Everett."

"Everett. Yes. Thank you, ma'am."

Pierce was writing herself a note. Then she straightened up. Her face seemed to relax a bit.

"Okay." She waved toward the door. "Let's go say hello to the baby."

* * *

The baby was awake, lying on his back in a boxlike crib. Jake and Alice craned their necks and peered down at him. His eyes, bright and blue, wandered back and forth, unfocused.

"Oh," Alice breathed, "he's beautiful."

His skin was a deep brown, like a fine wood, and he had plenty of brownish blond hair, a mass of wiggly curls.

"I think he's smiling at me!" Jake slipped his index finger under the baby's tiny hand.

"Six days old," Alice crooned, her face shining. "Such a fine boy!"

Ruby was beaming.

Alice looked at the nurse seated nearby. "May I pick him up?"

Pierce cut in. "Of course you can. He's yours. Or nearly so."

Alice leaned down and slipped one hand under his head, the other under his bottom, and lifted him out of the crib. She cradled him in her arms, and Jake, grinning crazily, moved around to keeping looking at his face.

"What will you name him?" Ruby asked.

Alice looked at her abruptly. "Oh my!" she laughed. "I hadn't even thought!"

Jake never took his eyes off the baby's face. "This probably calls for a very long series of conferences," he said, taking the baby's hand between his thumb and forefinger. Then he changed to a mock-official tone: "Do you have any opening recommendations, young man?"

The baby squeezed out a gurgle.

"Glur," Jake repeated. "Well, we can take that under advisement," Jake declared, "but frankly I don't think you're going to be happy with the name Glur very long."

Alice and Ruby were giggling like little girls. "Oh lordy," Ruby gasped.

With the LaSalle loaded up, one of the nurses wiped her eyes. The others smiled and waved. Dr. Pierce raised a hand in farewell but was too weary to smile.

Everett watched from an upstairs window. "Goddamn," he says to himself.

Alice, cuddling the baby in the front seat, couldn't hold back the tears any longer. "I can't believe we're coming home with a baby."

"It will start sinking in, about the first poop," Jake chuckled.

"Oh lordy," Ruby giggled again from the back seat.

Jake pulled the LaSalle into gear, and they began moving away from Finnegan. Alice turned suddenly toward Jake. "I didn't know you talked to a lawyer!"

"I didn't."

"Jake! You said——"

"Yes?" he answered, all innocence.

"You told her Ruby's eighteen. You told her she finished school. You told her you confirmed the law!" She wrinkled her nose. "You're terrible!"

"Sometimes, darling," Jake said, his chin jutting, "the facts are inadequate."

* * *

When they needed a break, they pulled apart and collapsed on opposite sides of the bed. She lay on her tummy, looking away from him. Finally her breathing slowed.

"This place is such a dump."

Everett moved himself to a sitting position. "You're okay with the sex here, I guess."

She pushed herself up to lean on her elbows, and lowered her head to smooth her short dark hair with her fingers. "How do you live like this?"

"You've made it so entertaining." He lit a cigarette. "I'm not here much. I prefer the crazy house."

"God, I don't know how you stand that either."

She rolled over and sat up next to him. She reached for her pack on the table next to her side of the bed.

"Finnegan. Now *that's* entertainment," he sneered.

She lit up and took a long draw.

"One adventure after another."

They smoked in silence awhile.

"Damnedest thing this week." Everett took a long draw on his cigarette.

"Hm." She stubbed hers out.

"Black girl got pregnant. No telling who did it."

"At Finnegan? You told me."

"Had her baby. The baby's not black."

"What?"

"And it's not white. He's got dark skin, and blond curls."

"Huh. Gimme a cigarette. I'm out."

"I thought they were shipping it out to Sangamon." He retrieved the package on the table next to his side of the bed and handed it across his body. "But then this guy shows up, white guy, with his wife, and takes the baby."

"Hm." She lit a match.

"It was a salesman. The rubber guy."

"Rubber guy?"

"He sells rubber stuff. Gloves and stuff. He put all new walls and floors in the rubber rooms. Finally, now, our rubber rooms are really rubber."

Paula twisted toward him. "I knew a rubber guy once. From Leland Supply?"

"Yeah."

"He's there a lot? At Finnegan?"

"Yeah, I guess. Does lots of business with Pierce. The boss."

"Well, well, well," Paula said to herself, "the nipple man."

Everett turned to her. "The hell you say?"

Paula stubbed out her cigarette and turned to him. "Nothing," she murmured. She pulled down the sheet to expose herself. "Come here."

18.

Nicholas Austin Valentine exploded the world. He whined and squawked and cried and demanded his parents' attention, and got it. He cooed and gurgled and burped and chuckled and chattered and the universe came to a standstill when he did. He drank heavily. He ate enthusiastically. He urinated at will, and pooped prodigiously, and gave his parents continuous opportunities for training in diaper-changing, diaper-washing, diaper-drying, baby-bathing, baby-drying, baby-dressing, and more. The house underwent a revolution of smells. Both parents were exhausted and ecstatic.

"You look quite terrible."

Jake slumped a bit in the chair next to Katherine's desk. "Honesty is the best policy."

"I hear you've become a father," she said with her British lilt.

"That must be why I look so bad."

"Hard work, is it?"

"Not hard work. Just lots of work."

"And how can I be of service, sir?"

Jake looked at her. Same high cheekbones. Same lovely lips. Elegant nose. He sighed heavily.

Katherine resisted the urge to roll her eyes. "I wasn't referring to that."

"I didn't say a word!"

"You hardly have to."

"Do you realize how often we've had this conversation?"

"Every time we quit," she said under her breath. She tapped a pencil. "You plopped down at my desk. How can I help you?"

"I need a slot on Fivecoat's calendar. I mean when his head will be clear. I need an hour to chew through some big things. Hiring."

"Ah, hiring," Katherine replied with a casual toss of her head. "Leaving us for the Great Beyond?"

"Huh? What are you talking about?"

"Running for the legislature? Aren't you too exhausted now, *Daddy*, to be a state representative?" Her British accent clipped the word into pleasant little pieces.

"Oh, that. No. I can talk to him about that anytime. It's not that big a thing." He looked at the floor. "God, Columbus would be relief. Time off!" He looked back at Katherine. "Who the hell told you?"

"Sammy Jessup."

"Gordon's kid? Yeah, I've talked with Gordon about it a couple times. What are you doing, dating Sammy?"

Katherine half-shrugged.

"Jesus! Sammy?"

Katherine's face dimmed. "And why not?"

"Just between you and me — he's an idiot."

"He's not an idiot, and furthermore, he's something you aren't."

Jake started to speak, but Katherine didn't stop.

"He's single."

Jake slumped further. "I gotta get more sleep. Just get me the time, okay?"

She was looking at the schedule book. "He's clear Wednesday after three."

"See ya then," Jake said, hauling himself up. "Thanks for the laughs."

"Cheerio," Katherine called as he walked down the hall.

* * *

Ruby hated her duties, but the equipment did make the work far easier than cleaning white people's houses. And she was astonished by the amount she was being paid for such ordinary tasks. In the deep of the night, with the shroud of sleep covering most everything in the building, she mopped floors, dusted window sills, scoured toilets, scrubbed down shower stalls, washed dishes in the same kitchen where she had first met Dr. Pierce. A patient might shuffle down the hallway. A minder would appear and disappear. The other maintenance workers had their duties. Sometimes she saw them, usually she didn't. Sometimes a patient made a shit-mess, which gagged her, but it didn't last long. The medical people might leave a supply area in disarray, who knows why, but this wasn't a complicated, sophisticated hospital operation. It was easy enough to put a blade back in its tray, or return a bottle of some pharmaceutical to its shelf, or a partial box of rubber gloves to its cabinet. Slide the drawer. Close the door. No worries. If she crossed the path of someone else on the night shift, there was only a quiet hello, nothing more. Usually a young white man was on duty, usually lounging in the kitchen, from what Ruby could tell. She knew enough to stay out of the bottom cabinet in there, where the liquor was supposedly hidden. It was no secret — the man didn't react if she walked in while he was drinking — but she had no reason to go snooping around.

The beautiful thing was, she could see Maddie. If she came early, or left late, she might catch Maddie awake, and they could take a walk together. At first, it was hell. Her throat tightened with anguish, as she processed the sight of her sister here, in such a place. She tried to talk to her, to tell her about her day, like before. But even talking about Nicky, his murmuring, his whining, his little legs kicking, all the things she loved about him — Ruby's heart groped through spasms of frustration and rage. Time after time, sitting at Maddie's side, Ruby wept with quiet grief. Yet Maddie was impervious. She seemed content. And before too long, Ruby was able to let go. To hold Maddie's hand, and lead her to the yard in the earliest light of day, maybe to sit for a bit. Maybe Ruby would talk, maybe not. But the day came when she realized what this was, these simple times, without progress, without any real action, without expectations, without any agenda but to be together. This was love.

And trudging home from the bus stop, it was easy to stop at the mission, to see Alice and Nicky. He was still small enough that Alice could bring him to work, and most days there was a grandma volunteering, a white woman willing to help with a brown baby.

"I'm Auntie Ruby!" she cried, holding Nicky on her lap.

"Yes, you are," Alice replied with a huge grin. "The best auntie in the world."

"Wah," Nicky said.

"You see?" Alice added. "Nick agrees."

"Wah," Nicky said again.

"Oh lordy!"

The baby smiled for Ruby, and wiggled his fingers.

"Ain't no domestic," Ruby murmured, taking his hands.

Alice looked up quizzically. "No what?"

"No domestic. My mama preached it. 'Ruby, stick in school. Don't be no domestic.'"

She was still grinning at the baby. "I can't be no domestic no more, cleaning folks' houses. Cleaning the crazy house, that's all right, I guess."

"Wah," Nicky said.

"What you gonna be, little Nicky?" Ruby sang. "You gonna be big and grown-up, and smart. You'll learn to read and write——"

Her face went grim.

"Alice?"

Alice was sorting papers. "Hm."

"Where will he go to school?"

Alice looked up. Her hands stopped moving. "I don't know."

Ruby was studying the baby's face. "He's so brown. Too dark for the white school. But these blond curls, lordy. He's too white for the Negro school."

Alice's face was a stone. "It's too early to worry about that."

Nicky burst into chatter. Ruby made big eyes at him. He laughed.

"Maybe by then," Alice said softly, "things will be different."

* * *

The baby was finally asleep, in the crib next to Alice's side of the bed, and she sank into the sheets on her back. Jake was just coming in from the bathroom. He slipped in on the other side and took her hand.

"I'm open in the morning, babe. I can get up with him. Let you sleep."

Alice thought about it. "We'll see."

"I hope to have more time pretty soon. I think Fivecoat is gonna let me hire a guy."

Alice smiled in the dark. "We'll see."

Jake tugged on her hand a bit. "What does that mean?"

"You'll need time for the campaign. And then for Columbus."

Now Jake lay still in thought. "That's not a sure thing yet."

Alice turned toward him and placed her hand on his waist. "I think you should run."

Jake's face pulled back. "You never said this before."

"I think you have to. There are things that need to change here. You persuade people."

Jake frowned. "What are you talking about?"

"Where will Nicky go to school?"

"What?"

"The white school? Or the black school? Who will have him?"

"Aw, Alice, you're worrying so early about this."

Alice ignored him. "There's shouldn't be a Negro school and a white school. There should be a Leland school."

Jake's voice grew high with tension, and his body bent toward her. "You want me to go to Columbus and convince the State of Ohio to put coloreds and whites together in all their schools?"

"Shh. You'll wake him."

"Alice." He slumped onto his back.

"It's happening other places. I read about it all the time. It should happen here."

Jake took in a deep breath.

"Ruby says the Negro school is terrible."

"I know," Jake replied, miserably.

"We never had to think about it before."

"I know."

"Now we do," Alice said. "It will be our problem soon. They say 'separate but equal.' But we know it doesn't happen that way. The only way for Nicky will be 'together.'"

Jake stared at the ceiling. "I know."

Alice waited awhile, but he didn't speak again.

"You have to run, Jake."

She couldn't tell if he was still awake, and then, with the release of one heavy breath, exhaustion caved in on her.

* * *

"Mr. Jessup," Jake began.

"Call me Gordon."

"Thank you, sir. How's your ankle?"

"Miserable." He shifted his weight uncomfortably on the couch, his jowls wiggling with the awkward motion. What's on your mind, Valentine? You don't look any too happy."

"I owe you some information."

"I'm listening."

"My wife and I have adopted a child. It came up rather suddenly."

"Well," Jessup said with steely balance, "congratulations."

"Thank you, sir. It's a boy."

"Good, good."

"But our baby is unusual."

Jessup studied him. "I'm listening."

"He's not white."

Jessup didn't flinch. He waited only a beat. "You adopted a Negro baby?"

"No sir. He's mixed-race. He's blond. But he's brown."

Jessup sat for another beat, then leaned over to massage his lower leg. "The hell you say." He didn't look up.

"I apologize if this puts you in a difficult position."

Jessup didn't answer. He finished with his leg, grunting a bit at the pain, and straightened up.

"I realize this could be a problem, sir. But I felt — my wife and I felt — that nobody would take this baby. The orphanage isn't good. Not good at all."

Jake hesitated, but Jessup was making no effort to speak.

"And in the end, as I considered it, I decided that — well," and he took a sharp breath — "people are people, and it shouldn't matter. That's——"

The two men stared at each other.

"That's what I believe. I'm sorry if it's a problem."

Jessup tossed his chin toward a cabinet. "Bring a couple whiskies."

Jake got up and moved.

"Goddammit," Jessup said, half to himself, shifting his weight again. "Well, Valentine, I told you we got nobody else."

Jake tried to be steady as he poured drinks, his back to his host, and kept listening.

"We won't make this a problem, goddammit. If it gets to be an issue, we'll make it a feature. Compassion. Equality. The things we stand for."

Jake delivered the whisky and sat back down. He watched as Jessup took a swig and scrutinized him. Jake prepared for the dressing-down.

"You're the real article," Jessup finally continued. His expression didn't change. He was dictating a press release. "You're the new wave. You actually believe. You do what you believe."

"I guess I do," Jake said. It felt vaguely strange to say it.

"No guessing," Jessup shot back. "From now on, you know what you believe, and you do it. That's what you say, and that's what you do. The new wave. And we sink or swim in it."

Jake sipped his drink. "Yes, sir."

Jessup threw back the last of his whisky and held the glass out. "Get me another."

Jake stood and took the glass to the cabinet.

"But no more problems, Valentine."

"No, sir."

"I still have Torrance and Claxton to get in line. Don't make this more difficult for me."

Jake poured. "No more problems." He turned with the whisky and handed it over. Jessup was still glaring at him.

"You're brave," he said, taking the drink. "Or crazy."

Jake sipped. "Both, maybe," he said quietly.

19.

Manray's, the function hall, looked great: dozens of bright red Christmas ornaments suspended from the ceiling, a fabulous tree in one corner, golden garlands cascading. A quartet played Christmas music near the tree — a string quartet, but with a guitar in place of the viola. On a long line of tables, covered with bright green tablecloths, were mountains of food: cakes and candies, fruits and cheeses, meats and nuts. A colored couple in white shirts and aprons were tending bar.

Dressed in reds and greens and blacks, a few in Santa hats, Leland Supply employees, colored and white alike, were clumped in threes and fours, drinks in hand, with children darting between the groups, a few sullen teens hanging together against a wall.

The roar of conversation, chatter and laughter, made Nicky blink as they entered the room.

"Oh!" Alice peeped. "He'll cry!"

Jake reached out to take him from her. "Nah, he'll be fine," he said, smiling. "He'll schmooze!"

"Jakey! What have you got!" It was Mrs. Geist, thick and pink.

"My son Nick is making his debut," Jake said, swinging him around so she could see. "And this is my lovely wife Alice."

Mrs. Geist's face flickered. "Ah, he's——" She glanced at Alice. "So little to be out in the cold!"

Alice smiled and reached for the baby's red and green knitted cap. "Actually, it's so warm in here, I think he'll be fine without this now."

"So you adopted," Mrs. Geist said, nodding to herself as she stared at Nicky.

"Yes, this little guy needed a home," Jake replied. "And I said, 'I know just the place!'"

Mrs. Geist was still nodding. "How old is he?"

"Three and a half months."

Her eyebrows knit together. "So small baby for such big party!"

"Hey," Jake said, giving her a shoulder, "everybody else brings their kids to Fivecoat's Christmas party. Why not me?"

Mrs. Geist finally snapped out of it. She looked at Jake. "Aw, Jakey, that's right! Why not!" She beamed and reached out to take Alice's elbow. "Congratulations, dear missus."

"Thank you," Alice replied.

"If you need wise advice, you come to me. Ursula Geist. I did this six times!"

Alice's face brightened. "Six times!" She laughed. "Yes, I will sure call you!"

And so it was, for an hour — a steady, noisy stream of introductions — each a copy of the last: the startled first look, the stammered well wishes, and finally the measured approval. From the white-skinned Mr. Svenson and his wife, from the black-skinned Mr. Feagle and his wife, from Mrs. Epperstein with her thick curly hair and her bald husband, and on and on.

In the chaos and clatter, they found Fivecoat.

"Mr. Fivecoat, I'd like you to meet the newest member of the Leland Supply family," Jake announced.

Fivecoat was dressed in the same enormous Santa jacket he wore every year.

"This is Nick Valentine."

Fivecoat held his scotch away while slipping an arm around Alice. "Hello, young lady. Congratulations."

"Thank you, Mr. Fivecoat."

He turned to inspect the baby. "And to you, Jake." His eyes fluttered almost imperceptibly. "I see," he hurried to say. "Well, welcome to the party — Nick, you say?"

"Nicholas Austin Valentine."

Fivecoat took a sip and looked from Jake to Alice. His cheeks were ruddy with scotch. He smiled warmly.

"You're brave people," he said. "I salute you."

Jake and Alice glanced at each other.

"Thank you, sir," Jake answered.

Fivecoat and Nicky looked at each other. Fivecoat tilted his head toward the baby. "This little fellow will have a fine life with these two good parents."

"Thank you, sir."

Fivecoat's face swung around. "Time for a refill. Get something to eat!"

"Do you want me to take him?" Alice asked, reaching under the baby.

"Yeah, I think my arms are about done with display duty," Jake said, handing Nicky over.

"Mr. Valentine." It was an English accent. They turned to see Katherine.

"Oh, hello," Jake said cheerily, reaching for a handshake. "Katherine Abbott, this is my wife Alice, and our son Nick."

"Very pleased to meet you," Katherine said with a polite smile to Alice. "And you." She took Nicky's hand. Her face jumped. "Oh dear!" she piped. "You're so beautiful and brown!" She caught herself, her eyes flashing at Alice. "I'm sorry. I was just so surprised."

Alice smiled and looked at Nicky. "It's all right. He is beautiful and brown."

"But those blond curls!" Katherine went on. "Oh dear. He's wonderful!"

Alice was smiling broadly. "Yes, he is. Thank you."

"Well," Katherine concluded, with a smile. "Congratulations to all three of you. Have a lovely evening."

She was off into the crowd.

Nicky squeaked a small complaint.

"We'll need to take him home soon," Alice said, close to Jake's ear.

"Yes. Okay."

"She's quite beautiful."

"Katherine? She runs Fivecoat's office like General Patton."

"I love her accent."

"Yeah. British, I think. You want anything else to eat?"

"No, I'm finished."

"We can't forget his bag."

"Of course not."

"It's on the shelf above the coats."

"Yes, I remember."

Nicky emitted a long squeal. Jake smiled. "The timer has gone off."

* * *

"I'd like to speak to Mr. Fivecoat, please."

"Thank you, may I tell him who's calling?"

British, Paula thought. *Very impressive.* "I really need to speak to Mr. Fivecoat privately."

"I beg your pardon, but I'll need to know who's calling before I'm able to put you through."

"Do you have a Jake Valentine working there?"

"I trust you understand my position. I'll need to know who's calling, please."

"He's got a new baby? A half-breed?"

"I beg your pardon."

"I think Mr. Fivecoat should know, that baby was born to a black girl, a patient at Finnegan."

There was a long pause.

"The crazy house."

"Thank you, I know what Finnegan is."

"Isn't Mr. Valentine a salesman of yours? Doesn't he spend a lot of time out at Finnegan? An awful lot of time?"

Now another pause, but shorter this time.

"I'd like to know who's calling, please."

"I think it's rather common knowledge that he's a ladies' man."

"This is not appropriate."

"You've probably found that out yourself, haven't you? Little miss Brit."

"I beg your pardon!"

"Look, sweetie. If it comes out that Jake Valentine was doing it with a crazy girl at your customer's place, don't you think Mr. Fivecoat will want fair warning?"

Another pause.

"Thank you for your call," Katherine finally said, and hung up.

* * *

The door swung wide, and Jake was one big smile.

"How's my boy!"

Alice smiled, spooning a bit of something orange into Nicky's mouth. "Kiss your wife," she said ruefully, pointing to her cheek.

"A cheek! You only offer me a cheek? Outrageous!"

He bent in half to place his face directly between mother and baby. "Lips! I demand lips!"

He gave her a peck and straightened up. "Much better."

"Ah, bah, bah," Nicky agreed.

"Six months!" Jake exulted. "Such a big boy!"

"Ah, bah, bah," Nicky agreed, and laughed.

"He's doubled his weight," Alice said. "He's a load!"

"He's the fearsome Giant Boy!" Jake cried, tilting left and right with his hands up, like a happy monster.

"Ah, bah, bah!" Nicky cried back.

Alice's eyes glittered as she guided another spoonful into Nicky's mouth. "Good day?"

"Yes, good." Jake pulled up a chair to watch Nicky's progress with the orange glop. "Happy customers, happy salesman."

"Good."

"Still trying to work out hiring a new guy. It's more complicated than I thought. The company's bigger, way bigger than when I started with them. What to pay him, how to pay him, contingencies, on and on. I'm tired of it. What is that stuff?"

"Ah, bah, bah," Nicky answered.

"Pumpkin," Alice said.

"It looks horrible."

"He likes it."

"I see that."

"Ruby was at the mission again today."

"Yeah?" he was pulling off his jacket.

"I hate to see her trudging all the way from the bus stop."

Jake was heading into the bedroom.

"Have you thought any more about what we talked about?"

"No," he called, out of sight. "How can we do that?"

"We could convert the back room. Or add a room off the kitchen."

"Alice." He appeared in the doorway. "We can't bring a black woman to live in this neighborhood. Not just to move in, like a tenant. She could be a domestic."

"We have Nicky!" Alice exclaimed. "Look at him!"

Jake tilted his head a little. "I think he's the limit."

Alice's eyes locked in on his. "He could be the start. Not the end. The start."

Jake raised his hands and fell into a chair. "Call her a domestic. She doesn't have to really be one."

"She has to *pretend* to be the *help*?"

Jake said nothing. Alice turned back to Nicky and offered another spoonful. He backed away.

"What am I going to say to Gordon Jessup? 'Guess what! We're taking a black girl into our house. No, not a domestic. Like a friend. Like family.'"

Alice glared. "She *is* a friend! She *is* like family!"

"He told me specifically: 'No more problems.' This is a problem, Alice. I can just hear him roaring. 'What the hell are you doing?'"

Alice was wiping the baby's face.

"I can't make a difference in Columbus if I don't get elected in the first place."

Alice was silent as Nicky dodged her rag.

"I can't get elected if I don't run. And I can't run without Gordon's committee people."

Alice lifted the baby and turned to Jake, her lips drawn in a stern line. "I know."

"It's not about Ruby," Jake insisted, standing up. "Ruby's fine." He opened a cabinet and pulled out a bottle. "It's just difficult."

20.

"This is very nice."

"And you are very nice."

Katherine looked shyly at her plate. "Thank you, Sammy. You're a dear."

She looked up. She could tell that the candlelight dancing on her face pleased him.

"I was only here once before," he said. "My father and some big shots. A political thing."

"Ah yes, big-shot politics," she said with a wry smile, and sipped her Manhattan.

Sammy shrugged. He was tall and thin, with black hair, wavy but cropped close, and gold-rimmed glasses. "It doesn't interest me much," he said. "But it looks like your company will be in the middle of it pretty soon."

"How do you mean?"

"Jake Valentine. Your star. I think my father and his people — that always sounds so pretentious to me: 'his people' — but anyway, it looks like they're about to get behind Valentine for the legislature. The house."

Katherine watched her finger as she drew it around an edge of her glass. "I see."

"My father says he could be the future. Especially with that kid they adopted. The half-breed, you know? 'Breaking down racial biases, in the second half of the 20th century!'" He made a face. "Et cetera, et cetera." He took a drink of his scotch. He arched an eyebrow. "Katherine?"

She looked at him.

"You seem to have something on your mind."

"I don't know," she replied, looking down at her glass again. "I mean, I do know. Yes, I have something on my mind. But I don't know what to say."

"About what? Jake Valentine?"

"Yes."

"I'm very fond of you, Sammy," she began, without looking up, "and I don't want something to happen that could embarrass your father, and then you discover that I could have——" She looked at him. "Warned you."

"Warned me? God. What is it?"

"It's only something I've heard. I have no way of knowing if it's true or not. Maybe it's rubbish. It sounds like rubbish."

"Katherine, please. What?"

"The baby Jake adopted might be his own."

Sammy's eyebrows bent above his glasses. "What?"

"I heard that the baby didn't come from an agency in Pittsburgh. It was born to a black girl at Finnegan."

"The crazy house?"

"Finnegan is one of Jake's accounts for us. For the company. He's there a lot." She took a drink. Sammy's mouth stood open. "It seems impossible. It's probably nonsense. I haven't even repeated this to Mr. Fivecoat."

"God," Sammy said, and downed his drink.

"But if you — if your father." She stopped. "Please don't tell him where you heard this."

Sammy drummed his fingers on the table.

"Are we ready to order?" said a thin, balding waiter in a bow tie.

Sammy raised one hand to him without looking at him. "Not quite yet."

The waiter withdrew.

"Then what do I tell him?"

"I don't know," Katherine pleaded. "Tell him you heard it from a friend, who heard it from a friend."

"God," Sammy said again.

"You don't think it's true, do you?"

"I have no idea," he replied. "How would I know? But truth isn't what matters in these situations. You know? It's the story that kills you."

They looked at each other, paralyzed.

"How well do you know him?" Sammy asked.

Katherine looked away. "He works there. I see him every day. But," and then she fell silent.

"Do you think he could have done it?"

"Oh my God, how could I know that?" Katherine replied, weakly. "What's the girl like? I don't know." Then she looked at Sammy again, with a helpless frown. "Maybe?"

His eyebrows lifted away from the tops of his glasses.

"Maybe," she said. And she downed her drink.

* * *

They met at Karney's, this time on purpose.

"Thanks for coming," Jake said, shaking his hand.

"Of course," Perry answered. "Long time."

"Hell of a long time," Jake said. "Too damn long, I know. I'm sorry."

"You're a busy man, Mr. Valentine."

"Well, thank you for that courtesy, Perry, but this isn't about me being busy."

"Well, I'm sure you'll tell me what I need to know, whenever I need to know it."

Rory was there. "What'll you drink?"

"Got Reingold?"

"Sorry."

"Hamm's, then."

Rory turned away to pour.

"It's just administrative crap," Jake said. "It's a big, complicated company now. Lotta growth. They're having to make stuff up as they go. Projections, compensation, all kinds of things."

"Of course."

"But I still think it will happen. Otherwise I wouldn't have wanted to check back in with you. I want it to happen. It will be good for me, and good for the company, to have someone else selling."

"Mr. Valentine, I very much appreciate this."

"Jake is okay with me," Jake replied.

Rory brought the beer, and a gin on ice for Jake.

"You told me what they're paying you at Finnegan. I know you can do way better with us. But the details, they just haven't put them all together yet."

"You should feel no pressure on my account," Perry said. "I'm ready to go. I'm ready to wait."

"Good. Thank you. When it happens, I know you'll succeed. It's not about learning a skill. I can teach you to sell in a week. A day. It's not about skill. Or even experience. It's personality. Instinct. I saw that the day I met you."

"Well, thank you — Jake."

"I'm working on it. Talking to Fivecoat, chipping away at the details. I just——" He gestured to the room. "That's why I wanted to meet you here, not at the plant. I don't want Fivecoat to feel like I'm getting ahead of him. Or pushing him, you know?"

"Sure. It's okay." Perry sipped his beer. "Anything I can do to help, just let me know."

"Stay patient. That's all."

"I'll stand by. Thank you."

"Thank *you*."

"Meanwhile," Perry said, with a partial smile, "back to the crazies."

* * *

Alice's head pounded. Nicky was whining from his crib, but she couldn't get up. Her legs were weak, folded under her, as she hunched over the toilet. Then came the wrenching again, from deep in her gut, and coiled up into the back of her throat, and she heaved into the brown, soupy water.

Can't be true.

Her face was slimy with sweat. Every breath scraped. The stench of her vomit rose from the bowl, and her stomach roiled again.

Can't be. No.

Her throat grabbed and twisted, and pushed another fistful up. The baby cried. She retched into the toilet, but nothing was left to throw up. She leaned on the edge, tears blurring her vision.

"It's all over town," the woman had said. "That explains a lot," the man had said. Loading boxes in the back of the mission, the volunteers didn't know she was standing there, just beyond the door to the warehouse. "Of course he had to adopt the child."

No. No. Jake wouldn't. It's crazy.

She reached for a towel. Swabbed her face.

He's changed. I've seen him change.

The sour taste in her mouth gagged her again. She tightened her stomach against the impulse to vomit. The calendar reeled backward in her mind. Nicky was eight months now. Nine months before that was, what? When? A year ago December? What was Jake like then? How was he acting?

He went along so easily with the adoption.

"Come here, sweetie, gimme a little kiss."

Her lungs were burning.

"That girl was beautiful."

He let me talk him into it.

"I oughta walk outa here and never come back."

Her temples were screaming.

"I've had plenty of women."

No. It can't be. It's just people being cruel.

"I don't need this aggravation."

It's Nicky's dark skin. People are mean. People are savages.

"I'll find me a good woman, goddammit."

Her stomach churned again.

Dear God, please let it not be true.

The baby wailed. Alice wiped her mouth and pushed herself to stand.

"Coming, darling," she called feebly.

She staggered a bit, trying to walk. She steadied herself against the sink.

"Stop this," she said to herself.

She put a hand against the wall and made her way to the crib. Nicky was standing, his face pinched. When he saw her, he stopped crying. A new wave of nausea swamped her.

Oh God. Does he look more like Jake every day?

21.

It was finally warming up in the second week of June. It would be perfect for a stroll around the grounds with Maddie before the night shift. Ruby stepped down off the bus, walked around to the back as always, went in through the kitchen, and left her things in a cabinet designated for the maintenance help. Then it was not much of a walk to the dorm where they kept Maddie.

Ruby opened the door carefully, slipped inside, and drew the door almost closed, so only the narrowest sliver of light from the hallway sliced into the dorm. An ugly harmony of snores arose from the beds. It always took a second or two for Ruby's eyes to adjust. She knew very well which bed was Maddie's, and she could make out the gentle mound of her body under its blanket.

But a rustle made her pause. In the hallway, the swoosh of fabric. Someone was coming. Ruby froze. It wasn't strictly forbidden for her to be here. Technically she needed someone on "patient staff" to bring Maddie out of the room. But no one had ever questioned her before. No one had ever brought the issue up. Yet something caught in Ruby's throat. She didn't want trouble. In that instant of calculation — *Who is it? Will they stop here? Will they care?* — she stepped aside, into a corner, into the dark, behind a dressing screen. The moment she did it, she knew it was a mistake. If whoever it was came in, and found her there, she would look guilty. *For no reason!* she shouted at herself in silence. *I'm not doing anything wrong!*

The soft steps slowed and ceased outside the door.

"Damn," a young man said quietly. "Who didn't latch this door?"

Heart pounding, Ruby could see the white man, Perry, using two hands to close the door behind him in complete silence. Moonlight leaking through the window shades at the opposite end of the room silhouetted him as he slipped his shoes off, leaving them at the door. He moved into the darkness. Through the narrow hinged gap between the two halves of the dressing screen, Ruby could follow his shape. He stopped at Maddie's bedside and reached under her blanket. Ruby's heart seemed to stop. She couldn't breathe. She couldn't look away.

He tugged at his trousers, then his outline bent and dropped into the outline of Maddie's covers. He said something quiet; Ruby couldn't make it out.

"Mm, mm," Maddie mumbled. "Bee, key."

The blanket rose and fell, rose and fell. Ruby screamed in silence, her eyes riveted on the motion, like a wave, faster now, and faster still, until Perry moaned, maybe a word or two, maybe nothing, and the awful wave died.

In a second he was bent over the bed, working at Maddie's pajamas. Then he straightened, with his hands at his own trousers, and in a flash was pulling Maddie's covers back up to her chin.

A rasp cut through the dark, and Ruby's body, clamped into stone, jolted with the shock. "Colored!"

Georgia, the bony old woman with one droopy eye, was propped up on one elbow. "Colored!" she screeched again.

Perry stepped to her, reached out to touch the back of her head, and bent to kiss her on the hair. "Easy now, Georgia."

He glided to the door, tugged his shoes on, and the light of the hallway roared in as he slipped out. He closed the door behind him with perfect silence.

Ruby's face was hot and wet, but the sweat was leaching off, leaving her skin cold and clammy. She shivered, and held herself, and then couldn't stop shivering. She was still behind the screen, still looking through the gap, but her body was convulsing, her vision was blurred with tears and rage and fear, so that the narrow vertical image was jittery. Her mouth was tight across her face, her throat was choking back the sobs. She hugged herself harder. She bit down on her teeth.

Slowly, oxygen returned to her brain. She tugged her breathing in, gulp by gulp, like a fisherman pulling up his nets. Her mind was wheeling and tumbling. She needed to think. She needed to get to work. She needed to die. She needed to run. She needed to scream. She needed to kill.

* * *

Alice had to pull herself together, and she did. *Insane*, she told herself, *insane to believe such a thing. Insane for anyone to do such a thing. Jake is smarter than that. Better than that.*

That evening, she came out of the bathroom to find Jake spread out on the floor, on his stomach, Nicky mirroring him, and each boy giggling at the other.

"Where is it?" Jake asked. "Where's the ball?"

Nicky reached for the upside-down cup and picked it up.

"There's the ball!" Jake crowed. "You did it!"

Nicky laughed, his blond curls bouncing, and picked up the gray rubber ball. Then he put it straight into his mouth.

"Blecch!" Jake winced. "Don't eat the ball. You're nine months old. It's time you learned the truth. Rubber is not food." He turned to Alice with a bright smile. "It's a difficult lesson, in this family, because we turn rubber into food."

"Yes, you do," Alice replied.

Jake took the slobbery ball from Nicky and wiped it on his shirt.

"That doesn't look too sanitary!" Alice called.

"Children have been eating dirt for centuries," Jake retorted, setting the ball back down and covering it with the cup. "Where's the ball?"

"Nah, bah, bah!" Nicky jabbered with glee, grabbing the cup.

"There is it! You did it!"

Alice shook her head, smiling. *How could this man be the man in the story? That awful story. It's not possible. Alice, you're terrible.*

"You boys," she laughed.

"Parenting is simple!" Jake proclaimed, taking the ball from Nicky's hand. "It's like the assembly line at the plant." He covered the ball with the cup. "Repetitive actions. Where's the——"

Nicky already had the ball, yelping with delight.

"Look at you!" Jake cried. "Now you hide the ball." He took the ball from Nicky's hand and placed it in its usual position. "Hide the ball," he coaxed. He handed the cup to the boy.

Grinning wide, Nicky scissored his arm and threw the cup to one side. Jake's face widened with surprise. Nicky laughed and reached out to take the ball in hand.

"What did you do!" Jake demanded with a laugh.

Nicky pushed his gums against the rubber.

Jake turned to Alice again. "There's something wrong with this child," he said. "He throws the cup, and puts the ball to his mouth."

Alice turned her head to one side and looked at her child. "I hope that's the worst problem he ever has."

That night, Alice slept poorly. Dreams woke her, but she couldn't remember them. The baby was a good sleeper. She could see the reassuring rise and fall of his blanket. She looked the opposite direction at Jake. *Also a good sleeper*, she said to herself. He was beautiful to her. Even with his hair tangled on the pillow like a badly made nest, even with his mouth ajar, she loved his cheekbones, his jawline, his nose. *This is a good time*, she insisted silently. *We have a beautiful baby. You have a good job. We have a lovely life.*

The next morning, she was nauseous again.

* * *

Ruby walked heavily from the bus station, past the mission. Her face felt slack on her skull, as if there were no energy left to hold an expression in place. She trudged along the street, her steps wearily mechanical. She was well beyond the mission, almost out of sight, when Alice, passing a window in the mission kitchen, noticed her receding form.

"Ruby?" she said aloud, as a reflexive response, with no one there to hear her.

Strange she didn't stop. Alice dried her hands on a cloth and hurried to the door. By the time she got there, Ruby was too far away to hear her. Right?

"Ruby!" Alice called anyway.

Ruby kept walking. She was a tiny bug now, each step a tiny pulse, disappearing into darktown.

Alice was just about to go back inside when her brain flared. She stopped, her hand on the doorknob. *She works there.* Had Ruby heard? Did Ruby believe it? *Oh, God, how awful.*

Alice opened the door and walked toward her desk, her mind spinning and sparking. *Does she know the truth?*

She didn't make it to the chair. Her stomach turned, and she lunged toward the bathroom.

Afterward, she tried to talk sense to herself. She would talk with Ruby about it. Tomorrow. When Ruby dropped by. Of course she would drop by tomorrow. It was just coincidence that she didn't today. She must have been tired. She had a hard night at work. Even if she heard the rumor, she wouldn't believe it. She knows Jake. She knows better. She knows.

Right?

* * *

"Mrs. Farris is sick."

"Mrs. Farris?"

"One of our volunteers. She's very good. I want to go see her this evening."

"Something serious?"

"I don't know. I just want to check on her. Express my support."

"Sure."

"I'll wait till Nicky's down."

"Okay."

"I don't think I'll be long."

"Okay."

Alice drove toward darktown, shaky with apprehension. Ruby hadn't stopped at the mission again this morning.

How long has it been since she skipped two days in a row? Maybe she's sick. Maybe that's all it is.

But what if it isn't? What can I say to her? What will she tell me?

Do I want to know?

God, do I want to do this?

Alice turned the corner onto Polk Street and stopped well short of Shirley's house. She took a deep breath, trying to quiet the noise in her head. It was a warm night. She rolled down a window. Maybe some fresh air would be good.

The high barking of an angry woman echoed through the night. Alice sat up straight. The vowels were arching like missiles, but at this distance the consonants were mushy, and she couldn't make out the words. "Though! Dough, heh, wah, hee!"

Then Alice realized she was hearing something both familiar and unknown: It was Ruby, and she was yelling.

Something slammed. Alice flung the car door open but thought clearly enough to close it quietly behind her. She hurried toward Shirley's house, where the front window, still missing half its frame, stood open in the muggy June night, its shade hanging torn and forlorn.

"Shush, Ruby," Shirley was saying. "Listen to me a minute."

Alice slowed her steps as the sound came clearer.

"Don't shush me," Ruby spat. "You ain't my mother."

"Stop that now. That ain't good for you."

Alice stepped to the corner of the house, and leaned her back against the peeling paint.

"I'll drink if I want to." Glass clinked. "I bought it."

"Ruby, you upset. But don't talk crazy."

"Ain't crazy!" she yelled. "He da crazy one!"

Alice's heart was drumming. *She can't believe that story. How could she?*

"Shush now!" Shirley begged. "What I say when neighbors come runnin'?"

Ruby brought the volume down. "Tell 'em cousin Ruby gonna take care o' him."

"Ruby, stop. What you think you gonna do?"

"Come on to Finnegan. Watch and see." Glass clinked again.

Alice grabbed her throat. *What will she do? What can she do?*

"Look, girl. You the wrong color, and you a girl. You can't pull down a white man."

"I'll find a way."

"You a fool."

"I seen what I seen," Ruby snarled. "I seen him do it to her."

Alice caught her breath, covering her mouth with her hand.

"Ain't your sister," Ruby went on, slowing to a growly drawl. "Maybe if you seen it, you don't care. I seen it, and I care." Glass clinked. "I gonna take care o' him."

"Ruby, hush now."

"He so high and mighty."

Alice's brain was a choir of howling.

"I'll take my time. But I'll find a way."

"Hush now."

Glass clinked. The voices fell silent. Alice's eyes darted in the darkness. Her legs felt wooden. She forced herself away from the wall of the house and stumbled toward the Ford. She flung herself into the driver's seat and then sat still, staring straight ahead, her hands tight on the wheel, her breaths coming fast.

"Come here, sweetie, gimme a little kiss."

God, please, no.

"Come on, don't you want a little kiss from your old man? Patty Connor likes to gimme a little kiss. Want me to go over to Patty's place and get a kiss?"

God, please. Is Jake real?

Alice's eyes finally trembled with tears. She suddenly realized her window was still open. She turned the handle to raise the glass. Then she lay her head back against the seat, and out came a sound she had never made before. It rose out of her soul and gushed forth.

When it was spent, Alice sucked oxygen till her chest stopped heaving. Then she reached for the ignition and turned the engine over. Her face was flat, like a field scorched and left to recover. Her throat was a dry pipe.

"Let her," she said aloud. "God's will be done." Her fingers gripped the wheel. "Whatever should happen, it will happen."

She put the Ford into gear and rolled away.

22.

"Dr. Pierce."

"Jake."

They shook hands.

"How's the baby?"

"He's good. Growing. Thank you for asking."

"Of course. I'm glad it's working out."

"Thanks for seeing me. I won't be long. It can be a very sensitive thing when a company hires someone who's working for a customer, so I'd like to get your blessing on something."

Pierce waited.

"I'd like to hire one of your night people. Perry Gavin. I don't think it will be a big problem for you here. But I think he can be a real asset to Leland Supply."

Pierce opened a file drawer. "Perry Gavin. It must be all right, because I don't even recognize the name."

"We haven't extended a formal offer to him yet. In fact, he hasn't interviewed with Mr. Fivecoat. I wanted to talk with you first, to make sure——"

"Oh yes. Here he is." She pushed the drawer shut and turned to Jake. "It's fine. Honestly, Jake, you could have just phoned me."

Jake smiled. "I wanted to extend every professional courtesy, dear doctor."

Pierce rolled her eyes.

"You're a valued customer," he insisted.

"Et cetera, et cetera," she smirked. "Nice to see you, Jake. Have a good day."

"Thank you. You do likewise."

* * *

Everett had just dumped himself into a chair in the kitchen, his shift finally ended, when Perry strolled in.

"You look awful goddamn happy," Everett grumbled, lighting a cigarette.

"Looks like I'll be taking my leave of the crazy house!" Perry answered energetically, sitting across the table from him.

"No shit. Where to?"

"I have an interview at Leland Supply. But the guy says it's basically a formality. I'm practically in."

"The rubber place?"

"Yeah."

"Well, hell," Everett intoned, reaching toward the bottom cabinet. "This calls for celebration." He brought out a bottle. "Escape!"

Perry retrieved two glasses from the upper cabinet.

"To escaping from Crazy Island!" Everett laughed, pouring whisky.

"To escaping," Perry echoed, smiling and lifting his glass.

They drank, and Everett poured again.

"Getting out," he said, almost pensively. "More power to ya. Hell, I hear that salesman from Leland has a scandal on his hands. You could be the top guy before you know it."

"Valentine?"

"Yeah, that's him."

"A scandal?"

"Folks are saying that kid he adopted outa here, he was actually the father."

Perry lowered his glass. "What the hell!"

"You know the kid was a half-breed, right? Dark skin, blond hair. But hell, I figure it coulda been most any one of the crazies in here. You can't police a place this big. You'd need an army."

Everett leaned forward to refill his glass. The outside door coughed open. Ruby closed it behind her and headed through the kitchen, looking at the floor.

"Hello," Everett said casually.

"Hello," Ruby responded, very quietly.

"I guess it's hello *and* goodbye tonight," Everett cackled at Perry. "This fine fellow is leaving us."

Ruby slowed awkwardly, not knowing how appropriate it would be to stop and talk — or not to. She stopped. "Leaving?"

"Well, not tonight," Perry said. "Probably a couple weeks."

"Got a job with some folks you know," Everett said with a toothy grin. "Mr. Valentine's takin' him on at Leland Supply."

Ruby stared dumbly at them.

"I see, well, that's nice," she finally said. "Well, I need to get working. Excuse me." She turned and left.

"She's all broke up about you leavin'," Everett snickered. "I guess the whole night shift's never gonna be the same without ya." He poured another. "Goddamn. Escaping from the crazy house."

* * *

No time.

With each slap and swish of the wet mop on the floor, Ruby silently recited the anxious mantra.

No time. He'll be gone. He'll be free. *Goddamn fucker'll be free.*

She squeezed the mop into the bucket. Her face was hot, knowing she was thinking words she would never say aloud.

Her brain clicked frantically as she worked. *Working for Jake, he could come back to Finnegan anytime. He could dance through this place like Jake does. Like he own it. Maddie will still—*

Then she jerked to a halt. She stopped breathing. Behind her eyes, she could see it.

It was a very simple idea. Hardly any sneaking. Hardly any hiding. But in the end, he would be done hurting Maddie.

For a moment, Ruby couldn't move. But the gears of her mind were grinding. *I can stop him.* Her breaths began coming, in pulses, like a signal. *I can protect her.*

Her brain and her body flicked back to the moment. Her breathing smoothed out. She finished the floor she was working on. She lugged her equipment to the medical supply room. On the counter was a box of rubber gloves. *Leland Supply*, the box said. She pulled three pair out, laid one pair on the counter, and stuffed another pair into the pocket of her work apron. She pulled the third pair on.

A wide tray held all the blades. She chose a scalpel, laid it on the rubber gloves, and carefully used them to wrap the blade, leaving only the handle exposed. Gently, she slid the little package, point down, into the other pocket of her apron.

Then she opened the cabinet and began inspecting the bottles. She knew what they used on the difficult patients. She didn't know how to say it, but she could read the label. She finally saw what she was looking for, and brought the bottle down: *Phenobarbital.*

The bottle wasn't big. She slipped it into the first apron pocket, and nestled it on the bed of rubber. She closed the cabinet, left the room, closed the door behind her. She pulled off the gloves. She didn't want to be seen wearing them. Maintenance workers never wore such gloves at Finnegan. She pushed the gloves carefully in on top of the wrapped scalpel. She picked up her mop and bucket and headed toward the kitchen. She wasn't scared. There was a tightness across her chest, but it didn't feel like fear.

She set down her equipment outside the kitchen. The door was open. She could see the legs of Perry's baggy pants stretched out under the table. Her brain began flashing. *Get him out of there – How? – Get him out – How? – Get him—* She took a single sharp breath, then walked in. He was sitting back in his chair, with a game of solitaire spread out on the table in front of him, and half the bottle of scotch, still open, and an empty glass.

"Sorry, sir," she said in a low voice. "Didn't mean to interrupt."

He waved coolly. "Not a problem."

"Feeling poorly," Ruby said. "Just thought I'd get some water."

Perry straightened up. "You sick?"

"I don't know," Ruby said, leaning deep over the sink, hands on the edge, elbows up.

Perry stood fast, scraping his chair on the floor. "God, don't give it to me." He whipped around the corner and out the door. "Some colored disease, all I need," he groaned as he fled.

Ruby listened to his footsteps retreating into the asylum. When they were gone, she slowly pulled the kitchen door closed and turned back to the table. Again she took rubber gloves out of her pocket and pulled them onto her hands. Then she reached in for the little bottle. Even through the gloves, it was chilly to the touch. Or maybe her hands were hot.

With her back turned to the door, concealing her work, she opened the little bottle and poured a bit into the scotch. She studied the side of the bottle. The scotch didn't look any different. There was just a bit more than before. She poured in some more, and inspected her work again. Just a little more. Then she closed the little bottle and returned it to the pocket. She pulled off the gloves, felt in her pocket for the scalpel, and tucked the gloves in beside it. She opened the kitchen door, picked up her mop and bucket, and went back to work.

She mopped another room, then another. The bucket swirled with clumped bits of paper, matted hair, insects. Again and again, she rinsed the mop into the bucket. For no reason, it occurred to her how strange it was that a floor could look so clean after being washed with such dirty water. Arriving back at the medical supply closet, she put on the gloves, opened the door, opened the cabinet, returned the little bottle to its shelf, closed the cabinet, left the closet, closed the door, pulled off the gloves, returned them to her pocket.

The tightness across her chest remained. She found herself clenching her teeth, and having to make herself relax them. When she finished the mopping, she didn't put her equipment away. She carried it with her, back to the kitchen. Perry was slouching at the table.

"God, are you still sick?" he blurted, bolting upright.

"No, I'm feeling better, thank you," Ruby said, leaving the mop and bucket in the hallway. She glanced at the scotch bottle. If he had taken any, he hadn't taken much. "Just another glass of water, and I'll go."

Perry half-snorted. "Jesus, the last thing I need is to get sick before this interview."

He reached for the bottle and poured. Ruby took a sip of water over the sink and looked around as Perry filled his glass.

She looked at the floor as she left the kitchen. "Excuse me, sorry," she murmured.

Ruby took her mop and bucket with her, but worked on window sills. Twenty minutes. She unclenched her teeth. Thirty minutes. She took steady breaths. She unclenched her teeth again. She picked up the mop and bucket and headed back to the kitchen.

As she approached the door, she could see Perry's legs splayed awkwardly, his feet turned in, under the table. Stepping in, she closed the door behind her. The glass on the table was empty, the bottle likewise. Perry's head was thrown back and cocked to one side, his cowlick like a buoy floating on the surface, his eyes closed, his mouth open, the back of his skull hooked on the back of the chair, his arms hanging at his sides, his shoulders moving up and down, slowly but steadily with his breathing.

Ruby took him by the shoulder and shook it a little. "Sir?"

His head wobbled a bit.

Ruby did not bother trying to unclench her teeth. She pulled on the rubber gloves and pulled the table away from him. Then she bent toward the elastic waistband of his baggy hospital pants and pulled the drawstring. The strings fell, lifeless. Using both hands, she reached above each of his hips and tugged the waist of his trousers down. Just an inch or two, that was enough.

With one hand she pulled the waist of the trousers away from his belly, his body jostling gently, and reached in. She was surprised that his penis was so thin and limp, almost less substantial than the cheap rubber of her gloves, as she pulled it up. His scrotum followed lazily. She tucked the waistband under it.

Ruby straightened up, felt carefully in her pocket, and brought out the scalpel. Holding it by its handle, she unwrapped the blade and returned the gloves to her pocket. The tightness across her chest was still there. But it was not fear. She looked at him, a ridiculous cartoon, passed out like a drunk, with his private parts squeezed up into a kind of bouquet, his balls bloated by the elastic, like a pair of bulging eyeballs, his penis a wrinkled balloon, lying wilted between them, like a limp nose.

It was not fear, but whatever it was brought the scalpel up. It took him by the tip and stretched him, long and thin. It pulled the blade through his flesh in a single swipe. What remained of him flopped back against the crease in his sac, and began oozing blood through his brownish-blond pubic hair, onto the globes of his scrotum, and into the fabric of his pants.

Ruby pulled his waistband back up into place, and the fabric fell against the severed stalk and began soaking with blood. Then she pushed the table back into position, took his left wrist and propped his hand on his belly. She slid the severed penis between his thumb and fingers and closed them around it. She brought his other hand up to the tabletop and placed the handle of the scalpel between his thumb and his forefinger.

She picked up the mop and the bucket and headed out back. Took off the gloves. Stuffed them into her pocket. They would go into the huge bin, with all the other medical garbage, at the back.

She dumped the dirty water, just like always, into the storm drain at the back corner of the property. Then it was time to put her equipment away and head home. End of her shift. End of her work week. Two days off now.

The tightness was still there, across her chest. But she could relax her jaw.

23.

Alice couldn't sleep. The baby couldn't either. She left Jake sleeping, dressed herself, dressed and fed the baby, and prepared to head to the mission.

"It's early," Jake said from the bedroom.

"Yes, sorry." She heard him rustling. "You don't have to get up. I'm sorry I woke you."

"It's all right, I need to get going. I have paperwork left over from yesterday, and I gotta get to Finnegan today."

"Bah, bah, pah, pah," Nicky babbled as Alice buttoned his top.

Alice took a breath at the name of the place. "Finnegan?"

"Got an interview with Fivecoat with this guy I want to hire; he works at Finnegan."

"Can't you call him?"

"Pah, pah, pah," Nicky answered.

"He doesn't have a phone at home." Alice could hear him sliding hangers on the rail in the closet. "I thought everybody had a phone at home by now."

"White people," Alice replied.

"Well, he's white," Jake said, pulling out a pair of pants.

At the mission, she situated Nicky in the extra playpen they had installed there for him, and sat down at her desk. She did not want to work. She wanted to cry.

And she needed to throw up.

She was bending over the toilet as Ruby walked home outside.

Ruby passed the mission without looking up. Her face was slack, but her chest was tight.

* * *

Pierce fumbled with a cigarette. Her office was already foggy with smoke. She couldn't get the match to strike. Standing, Everett leaned over her desk and lit it.

"Thank you," she said sternly, and took a long drag. She pushed the smoke out fast through her nostrils. "Jesus, what a mess."

Her free hand was shaped like a claw, her fingers on the desktop. She was forcing them to hold still.

"Well, it was *me* who took care of him," Everett pointed out. "And yes it was."

Pierce scowled down at the cigarette between her fingers.

Everett shrugged. "Although not really a lot of blood. I'm surprised. His pants sopped up a lot of it. He must have clotted up pretty fast."

Pierce rubbed her forehead.

Everett arched an eyebrow and sucked on a cigarette of his own. "More a mess mentally, I'd say."

Pierce shot a look at him.

"Well, he was screaming when I found him, screaming when I put the jacket on him, screaming when I dragged him into the rubber room, screaming when I closed the door. But he was losing some steam by then."

"God."

Everett grinned. "I thought you'd want some time to figure out how to handle things."

Pierce was frowning into space.

"Calling the cops seemed like a mistake."

Pierce dropped her hand from her forehead to the desktop. "Yes," she said sharply. "Thank you for that. No authorities. Nothing official. He stays in the room."

"He needs the rubber walls now anyway. He's gone nuts." Everett flicked ash into the ashtray on Pierce's desk. "Who could blame him, after that?"

"We don't know anything about how it happened," Pierce said, staring at what was left of her cigarette. She took another hit; her words came out in gray puffs. "So, nothing happened."

Everett smiled a cockeyed smile. "Who do you think did the 'nothing'? A patient? Staff? You don't really think he did it to himself, do you?"

Pierce glowered at him. "A drug addict gets drugs, gets crazy, and does something crazy to himself. It doesn't matter. Nothing happened. This absolutely cannot get out."

Everett half-bowed. "Of course." He tossed what was left into the ashtray, then sauntered to the door frame, leaned back against it and crossed his arms.

Pierce's eyes flickered with new alarm. "Will his family come looking for him?"

"I think he told me his father might have got the gas chamber. I think his mother ran off."

"You *think*?"

"All right, I'm sure. He didn't seem to have family. He was a loner. A crazy loner."

Pierce pushed her stub into the ashtray.

"A crazy loner who mutilated himself," Everett continued, looking around absently.

"That story will never need to be told," Pierce said with quiet force.

Everett shrugged again and lit a cigarette.

"I'm serious. He stays in the rubber room. He's a danger to himself and others."

Everett half-nodded.

"You get to staff," Pierce barked. "Everyone in the building. You make sure they don't know anything, or haven't heard anything. Or if they have, that they understand — nothing happened. This doesn't get out." She bit her lip. "I already spoke to Benson. She'll be okay. She's medical. Rules. Confidentiality. But the others, maintenance and—"

"The morning people have already left."

"Well, talk to every one of them tomorrow then." She put one hand to her forehead again. "God."

A pair of light thumps sounded at the door, and it opened halfway.

"Sorry, Doctor," Erma said, her face angled with worry. "But Jake Valentine is here to see you."

"Oh God, I forgot." She flattened her hand against the desk. "Uh—"

"Thank you, Erma," Jake half-sang with a broad smile, his hand on her elbow as he guided her to one side and opened the door the rest of the way. "I won't be long. I just—" Seeing Everett, his face changed. "Ah, forgive me, my mistake. I thought it was my time."

Pierce stood up with an iron face. "Jake, we've — My apologies, we've had a chaotic morning. Honestly, I forgot about you."

Jake raised both palms. "Not a problem, I don't need to interrupt you. I just wanted to talk with Perry Gavin — he doesn't have a phone — I need to set up his interview with Mr. Fivecoat."

Pierce reacted severely for a split-second, then her face seemed to go blank. Everett glanced at her without a flicker of emotion. Erma retreated, closing the door softly behind her.

"Perry Gavin," Pierce repeated.

"Yes, we talked about our hiring him," Jake said with an easy smile. His head bobbed to encourage her. "You said it was all right."

Pierce looked at Everett and back at Jake, and took a breath as she reached for another cigarette. "Gavin doesn't work here anymore," she said.

Jake's face clouded. "What?"

Pierce looked at the cigarette. "He didn't show up for work."

Jake frowned deeply and looked around the room, as if searching for an explanation. "He — I—"

Everett stepped toward the desk and stubbed out his cigarette. "Hmmm. When did you talk to him last?"

Jake fumbled. "Two — no, three — no, two days ago, I guess." He finally settled his eyes on Pierce. "No, three days ago."

Everett knocked another cigarette out of its package. "We haven't seen him since then," he intoned, and struck a match.

Pierce cleared her throat. "Jake, I'm sorry, but we really need to get back to work here."

Jake squinted in confusion. "Sure, I'm sorry to interrupt."

Everett moved behind him to open the door. "If he turns up, I'll tell him you asked for him. But I get the feeling he's gone."

Jake's face fell, like a serious schoolboy disappointed by his grade. "Sure," he said, turning to go. "Thanks."

"Sorry," Everett said, closing the door.

Pierce was lighting her cigarette. "God."

"Okay," Everett said. "It'll be okay. I'll get started with the staff. I'll take care of it."

Pierce dropped into her chair.

"I'll put the fear of God in 'em," he snarled, smiling. "After that, you got nothin' to worry about." He turned toward the door.

"Nothing," Pierce echoed, looking at her free hand. It was a claw again.

"A guy goes crazy, you put him in a rubber room," Everett said with a final shrug. "What could be more natural?"

* * *

At mid-afternoon the mission was stuffy, even with all the windows open. Nicky was sleeping. Alice opened the front door and stepped out onto the front landing, then sat down on it, her legs dangling over the side of it. She could almost see the playpen through the front window. She closed her eyes, grateful for a settled stomach. She prayed for a breeze.

Three young boys, two black, one white, came capering from around the corner of Golden's, the paper goods store at a diagonal across the street. They were in full summer vacation mode, oblivious to Alice; they were prancing and chattering and laughing as they grabbed at each other's crotches. Alice found herself wondering how well these three would get along thirty years down the line.

"Did too! I heard my mama say it!"

"Who?"

"Where'd she hear it?"

"She and her friend works there mornin's. They was talkin' about it when they got off the bus."

The third boy was trying to follow. "At the crazy house?"

"Yes! Cut off his pee-pee!"

"Who?"

"They found him like that!" One boy, grinning savagely, grabbed for another's zipper. "I'll show you!"

The boy squealed and pulled away. All three screamed with laughter and ran circles to escape each other.

"Who?"

"Cut it off!" one squeaked. "Really?"

"Yes!"

"Who?"

"A white guy! At Finnegan!"

"When?"

"This morning! I told you!" He grabbed for the other's zipper again. "Here, I said I'll show you!"

The three went tearing down the street. "Don't you want me to show you?" one yelled at the others.

Their laughing voices receded. The air hung sultry and still, but Alice shivered.

She rubbed her arms.

It's just boys, playing.

Her skin was bumpy.

Making up awful stories.

She stood up and went inside, picked up the phone and dialed Leland Supply.

"This is Mrs. Valentine. Is Jake Valentine available?"

"I'm sorry, ma'am, he's out visiting a customer."

Alice's brain crackled. *What did Ruby do?*

"Can you tell me where I might find him?"

There was a pause. Her tongue was dry.

"It's quite important."

"Well, normally we wouldn't give out such information, of course——"

Alice was having trouble catching her breath. "I understand that. I'm sorry."

"But since it's you, Mrs. Valentine, I'm sure it's all right to tell you."

God, what did Ruby do? "Thank you."

"The schedule book shows he was at Finnegan this morning, and then he was going to Zanesworth's."

"Finnegan."

"Yes, this morning, and then Zanesworth's, over in Verbena."

"Thank you," she murmured, and hung up. "Mrs. Farris?" she called, clomping urgently toward the back of the building. *Thank God she came in early.* The woman looked up from the box she was packing. Nicky gave a cry from the playpen. "Would you stay with Nicky, please? I need to run an errand."

Mrs. Farris's face brightened. "Of course, dear."

"I'm sorry, I woke him," Alice said breathlessly. "I'll try not to be long."

"It's all right, dear." Mrs. Farris was moving toward the front room.

Alice dashed past the playpen. "Mommy will be back, baby. Be good for Mrs. Farris." She could hear Nicky as she scurried to her car.

"Maa! Maa!"

The engine roared on the road to Finnegan. Alice's fingers gripped the wheel, and her neck muscles were tight. In the rear-view mirror she could see clouds of dust billowing and nothing more. She saw one car coming the other way, just outside of town, then none. The road was rural, and sadly in need of care. She was moving too fast to avoid the gaps and potholes. The Ford bellowed and bounced with each impact.

Then, in the distance, she saw another car heading toward her. In seconds it grew bigger and blacker. Big round headlights, like eyeballs, and a tall, narrow nose for a grill. Alice leaned into the steering wheel, looking hard at the oncoming vehicle. Her foot eased up on the gas as a black LaSalle roared toward her in the other lane. At ten car lengths, she saw puffs of dust explode off the back tires, and then again, as the driver pumped the brakes. By the time the Ford was racing past the LaSalle, Alice and Jake were gaping at each other with bewilderment.

She pressed the brake pedal and pulled off the road. There was too much dust to see behind her at first, but as it blew away, she could see in the side-view mirror that the LaSalle had also pulled over. She looked for traffic and swung the Ford into a U-turn, giving it gas to move into line behind the LaSalle. Jake was standing next to the open door, smiling quizzically, his hands on his hips. She threw the Ford into park and jumped out.

"What the hell, Alice!" he was shouting.

She raced to him and threw her arms around him, burying her face against his neck.

He held her tight. "What's going on, babe?"

Alice was breathing too hard to speak.

"Hey," he said softly, pulling her away.

Her face was hot, red and wet. She looked into his eyes and blinked a couple times.

"I'm crazy, I guess," she said, choking on a bit of a laugh. "I just needed to see you."

And she crushed him close again.

Jake didn't let go. "Are you all right? You don't seem all right."

Alice talked into his shirt. "I'm all right."

"Where's Nick?"

"Mrs. Farris has him."

He kept holding her. Finally she relaxed. She moved her face back to look at him squarely.

"I love you," she said.

Jake couldn't shake the puzzled expression from his face. "I love you too." But it was almost a question.

Alice breathed deep. "I have to go see Ruby."

"Ruby," he repeated, confused.

She pulled away. "I'll be all right. I love you." And she was hurrying back to the Ford.

"Hey!" Jake called after her. "I'll be late, remember. I'm having a drink with Jessup. Just drinks, he says, but you know how he does."

"All right," Alice called back, opening her door.

Jake stood there, watching her climb in.

"Hey!" he called again, his eyes twinkling. "You're a very interesting person!"

She poked her head out the window. "It's all the reading!" she called back, and gunned the engine.

24.

Even in the bright summer sunlight, Alice felt gloom, and trembled as she approached Shirley's house.

At the door, she knocked timidly. There was silence, then the torn window shade bent back, then hung limp again. A clank on the other side of the door, and it squeaked open a bit. Shirley's face partially appeared.

"Shirley," Alice said.

Shirley just stared.

"It's me. Alice."

Shirley did nothing.

"May I please come in?"

Shirley stayed still.

"Just for a moment?"

Shirley looked at her a couple seconds longer, then the door opened fast.

"Come in quick."

With the door closed behind her, Alice's eyes adjusted to the dim interior. Bags and boxes were scattered at random, some half-filled with clothing or kitchenware.

"Where is Ruby?"

Shirley eyed her warily. "She gone."

Alice's face melted into pleading. "Gone where?"

Shirley's hand was still on the doorknob. "I don't know. She wouldn't say."

"Wouldn't say?" Alice felt her eyes watering. "Where do you think?"

Shirley looked away.

"Shirley, please."

Silence.

"Please."

Shirley held onto the doorknob. "She said better you don't know."

Alice hung her head and turned away. "Oh God."

Shirley stood still. Alice looked around the room.

"You're leaving?"

"There's trouble."

Alice stared back into her face. "What kind of trouble?"

"I don't know. But if it's trouble, I don't want no part."

"Where will you go?"

Shirley looked away again. "Can't say. I got family."

"Shirley. Listen to me. If I can help, will you contact me?"

Shirley said nothing.

"If I can help, contact me. You can come to the mission. Or call there. Anything."

Shirley stood still.

Alice glanced helplessly around the room again. "All right," she said, turning to the door.

Shirley didn't hesitate. She opened the door. Alice took a step, then turned back to her. "Anything," she repeated.

Shirley said nothing. Alice turned to go. She heard the door close behind her, and the clunk of the bolt.

* * *

"What the hell."

Jake tossed his hat on the kitchen table and pulled the door hard.

"What — in — the — hell."

Nicky flexed his legs, holding on to the bars of the playpen. "Daa, daa, daa, daa, daa, daa!"

Jake fell into a chair and banged an elbow against the kitchen table.

"You should have been asleep already, young man," Alice said to Nicky, without smiling. "And now that Daddy is home, it will take forever." She lifted Nicky and nuzzled his neck. "Please sleep for me, Nicky," she said quietly. "I'm so tired."

"Jessup has gone weird on me. He was hot, hot, hotter, then today — bang. He's cold."

Alice swayed with Nicky in her arms. Nicky reached a hand toward Jake.

"About running?"

"Yes, about running!" Jake shot back. Then, just as quickly, he raised a hand. "I'm sorry. I'm not mad at you. I'm just—" He stood. "I'm screwed, I guess."

Alice swung the baby away from him. "And your son, learning to talk!" she yelped. She carried Nicky toward the bedroom.

"Daa, daa, daa, daa!"

Jake poured a glass. "We have some complications, he says. Some members of the committee have concerns, he says. Concerns."

"Let me get him down," Alice said from the bedroom, "and then we can talk."

Jake followed her to the doorway. "And my guy at Finnegan? The guy I was set to hire? He didn't show up for work. I don't know what the—" He shook his head and took a swallow.

Alice reached with one arm to turn off the lamp, and kept swaying with the baby. "Jake, please."

"Yeah, sorry." He turned, then turned back. "Here, I'll do it."

"Daa, daa, daa!"

"No, it's fine, you relax," Alice replied. "You've had a hard day."

"Daa, daa, daa!"

Jake set his drink on the dresser and reached for Nicky with a broad smile. "Look! He's calling me by name! How could a guy resist?" He took Nicky out of Alice's arms. "It'll relax me to put him to sleep. Who knows, maybe I'll put us both to sleep."

"Daa, daa, daa, daa!"

Alice kissed Nicky on the forehead and slipped out of the bedroom, pulling the door behind her.

"Okay, buddy, what shall we sing tonight?" she heard Jake say. Then he began to sing an old Ink Spots hit, softly and very slowly.

"May ... be ... you'll ... think of me..."

Alice looked at the baby mess in her kitchen.

"When you ... are all ... a ... lone..."

She twisted the faucet for hot water.

"Maybe ... the one who ... is waiting ... for you ... will prove ... untrue ... Then what will ... you do?" He let out a heavy sigh. Jake always took a heavy sigh there, trying to get the baby to give up. *"May ... be ... you'll sit ... and sigh..."*

Alice checked. It wasn't hot yet.

"Wishing ... that I ... were ... near ... Then..."

Alice checked the hot again, then turned on the cold.

"Maybe ... you'll ask me ... to come back ... again..."

She got the temperature set and plugged the sink.

"And maybe ... I'll say ... May ... be."

She scooped up flatware from dirty plates on the counter and reached for the soap. A soft rap at the kitchen window made her jump. The spoons clattered into the sink. Two dark eyes peered in from the dusk. A tiny cry creaked out of Alice's throat.

"Ruby!"

She raced to open the door. "Ruby!"

Ruby stumbled in, reeking of sweat and dirt. Her clothes were filthy, damp and limp. Her face was smeared, her hair frizzy. She had a worn basket in one hand, a small tattered suitcase in the other.

"I'm sorry," Ruby mumbled.

Alice's face was lined with alarm. "Sit down here." She closed the door. "What happened to you?"

Ruby set her things on the floor next to the door. "I tried to wait till dark," she said, looking at the table, "but the sun stays up, and I got too hungry."

"I'll get you something," Alice said quickly, spinning toward to breadbox.

"May ... be ... you'll ... think of me..."

Ruby looked at Alice wearily. "Nicky still up?"

"When you ... are all ... a ... lone..."

Alice tried to smile as she assembled what she could from the pantry and the refrigerator. "The days are so long, the sun never goes down, he doesn't want to sleep."

"Maybe ... the one who ... is waiting ... for you ..."

Ruby looked at the food.

"...will prove ... untrue ... Then what will ... you do?" A heavy sigh.

Alice put a clean plate in front of her, a knife and fork. "Please eat. Would you like milk to drink?"

"Yes, please," Ruby said quietly. She bit into a piece of bread without waiting to butter it.

Alice poured milk, sat in the other chair, and leaned toward her.

"Please, Ruby, I've been so worried. What happened?"

"I been hidin' today. I got in some trouble." She took a deep gulp of the milk.

Alice pleaded with her face. "Will you tell me about it?"

"Trouble at my job. I thought I better leave town. I only went back to Shirley's place to get my things." She took another bite of dry bread.

"Here," Alice said, reaching for the knife. "Let me butter you a slice."

"Thank you."

"But you're here now," Alice said as she worked. "I'm glad you're here."

Ruby lowered her head.

"If there's trouble," Alice said, "we will take care of you."

Ruby's eyes glassed with tears. "I couldn't leave without seeing Nicky one more time."

Her eyes closed, her mouth stretched tight, and her head began bobbing with silent sobs.

"Oh Ruby," Alice said. She knelt beside her and slipped an arm around her. "You don't have to go anywhere."

"I do, I think I do," Ruby answered, grinding the words.

"No," Alice insisted, reaching across to take her wrist. "You can stay here tonight."

"I don't think so," Ruby cried quietly. Tears dripped onto the wrinkles of her skirt.

"I'm sure it will be okay," Alice replied. "We'll talk about it in the morning. With Jake. We'll figure something out. You're exhausted. You need to eat, and you need to sleep."

"I can't stay."

Alice took her arm. "If you leave, what about Maddie? You won't see Maddie."

Ruby took a couple short breaths. "I can't stand to see Maddie like that no more." She looked away from Alice and took one more deep breath. "But Maddie's all right now. Nobody gonna hurt her no more."

Alice squeezed her arm. "Ruby, you stay here."

Ruby's face crunched with pain. "I'm sorry to bother you," she sobbed.

"Oh, Ruby, please." And Alice finally had to let her own tears flow.

Ruby reached around her, and they hugged each other tight.

Jake stepped into the room. Alice looked up, red-nosed, and sniffed.

"Ruby needs to stay here tonight."

Jake blinked dumbly. "Absolutely."

25.

With Ruby cleaned up and sleeping on the couch, Alice slips into the bedroom and out of her clothes.

"What is this?" Jake whispers.

"In the morning," Alice whispers back.

"Alice."

"Please. I don't want to wake the baby. Ruby needs to sleep. I need to sleep."

"She looked a mess."

"Something bad happened at Finnegan. I don't know what. She's afraid."

Jake stares unhappily into the dark. "Finnegan?"

"I heard some boys in the street, laughing about someone getting hurt."

"Hurt?"

Alice hesitates. "I don't know. It was little boys. Giggling. Maybe it was nothing. But Ruby doesn't want to go back there."

Jake traces the corridors of Finnegan in his mind. His first, furtive tour. The whisper of the floor tiles. The doors, identical sentinels lining the corridors. Brown Maddie, sleeping beauty, in repose. White Perry Gavin, blond angel, materializing at his side. *These folks get nervous with visitors.* The click-clack of the door to the supply closet. The dreaded mouthpiece. *We just call them thongs.*

A worm of apprehension slithers in his skull.

"Did Ruby do something?"

"Do something?"

"At Finnegan?"

Alice lies still.

"Something bad?"

Alice breathes in heavily, then out again. "I don't know."

The summer night hangs motionless. Jake walks the halls of Finnegan. Smells the oil rubbed into the hardwood bannisters. Tastes the ammonia in the air.

"I don't care," Alice says.

The summer crickets begin chirping in rhythm.

"She could come work with me at the mission. But she'll still need a place to live."

Jake flinches back to the moment.

"What happened to her aunt?" A little too loud.

"Shh."

"Or cousin, or whatever?"

"There was a problem there too."

"Geez."

Gordon Jessup's grim face hangs in the darkness. *I can't get the support, Jake.* He won't look Jake in the eye. *Torrance and Claxton are negative.* Jessup throws back a drink and pours another. *Is this about my son? Not being white?* Jessup scowls and shakes his jowls. *No, I told you that wasn't a problem. It's—* Jessup drinks again. *I got nothing more for you, Jake. We're not going to do it. Sorry.* He still can't look Jake in the eye. Jake mutters thanks and goes out.

His mind is cramped with questions. What happened? He re-runs the earlier meeting. *"The real article." "The new wave." "You do what you believe."* The statehouse in Columbus rises up in the dark before him, its line of soldierly columns standing solemn, barring entry, the cylinder of the rotunda looming overhead in scolding silence. Only Jessup's gravelly growl. *We're not going to do it.*

Jake sighs and rearranges the pillow under his head. He pushes the statehouse out of view. Leaves Finnegan behind. Swivels his mind to home. To now. To tomorrow. He feels Alice's body rising and falling with each breath. Imagines the outline of his son in the crib. Smells the silky summer air hovering at the window. Thinks of Ruby — wretched-faced, shiny with sweat.

Yes, we are going to do it.

* * *

What.

Sleep shattered. Ruby jolted. She needed a moment to remember where she was. *Alice's. Safe. For now.*

Her head began to swirl. She could see Perry Gavin, his mouth agape. See his sleeping hand, holding his prize. Trousers turning crimson.

Where will I go? Shirley won't take me. Back to Uncle George and Aunt Lela? Please, no. Where?

She pictured the bus from Pittsburgh, but now it was carrying her away. Destination unknown. Out the window, the earth growing crusty and dry. A desert moon. A hell of desolation.

And she pictured Maddie, cooing softly in her bed. A gentle half-smile on her lips. Now getting smaller. Drifting. Gliding from life into memory. Slipping away.

Ruby's mouth opened on a choke. *No! No, Maddie, no!*

She reached for Maddie's forearm, held it fast, pulled her back. Larger and closer, Maddie's head bobbing contentedly. Ruby gritted her teeth.

I will come back to you. Her eyes burned with tears. *I can't leave you all alone there.*

She tightened her throat against her sobs.

But where can I go?

* * *

"Alice."

"Go to sleep. Please."

"She needs to stay here."

Alice was silent for a bit. "Ruby?"

"She could live here. If she wants to."

Alice propped herself up on an elbow. "As the help?"

"Daa, daa," Nicky said.

Jake looked over Alice's shoulder at the crib. Nicky was standing. "Now look what you did," he said, frowning toward Nicky. "You want *me* to be quiet, and then *you* wake him."

"Daa, daa," Nicky repeated.

Alice rolled away from Jake and put her feet on the floor. She took Nicky in her arms.

"What about the statehouse?" she asked.

Jake put his hands behind his head. "If Jessup's gone cold on me, what the heck? I'm dead anyway."

Alice swayed. "He could change his mind."

"Daa, daa," Nicky said.

"Shh," Alice replied. "You need to sleep."

"What if he does," Jake answered. "Ruby will still need a place."

Swaying, Alice looked at him.

"Not as the help," Jake added.

Alice said nothing.

"It shouldn't matter," he said. "To white people. It shouldn't matter where people live. We can handle the neighbors, if they have a problem."

There was a long lull. Crickets chirped some more.

"We can fix up the back room," he said. "Maybe save up, and build out, past the kitchen."

Alice listened to the crickets awhile. It was warm in the dark.

"If she wants to stay," Alice finally said.

"Daa, daa, daa," Nicky said.

"I can probably talk her into it," Jake said drily.

Alice looked Nicky in the eye as she rocked from foot to foot. "Mister, aren't you ever going to sleep?"

"Daa, daa, daa, daa."

"Here, I'll do it," Jake said, crawling across Alice's side of the bed. "What'll we sing, buddy?"

He stood and took Nicky out of her arms. Alice slipped back into bed and watched them. Jake looked into Nicky's eyes as he gently swayed and sang.

"*May ... be ... you'll ... think of me ... when you ... are all ... a ... lone...*"

"It's good timing, I think," Alice said, "if she'll stay."

"*Maybe ... the one who ... is waiting ... for you ... will prove ... untrue ... Then what will ... you do?*" A heavy sigh.

"Actually, I might need some more help around here," Alice said.

"*May ... be ... you'll sit ... and sigh...*" Jake turned his face to Alice with a smirk. "I'm not enough help for ya, huh?" He turned back to Nicky. Nicky's eyes were closed.

"*Wishing ... that I ... were ... near ... Then...*"

"Because I think we're going to have a baby."

Jake's swaying slowed to nothing. Alice saw his shape bending, lowering Nicky into the crib. Then he stepped around the foot of the bed and climbed in on his side. He slid one arm around behind her neck, and reached the other across her body. His hand lay on her breast. She recoiled a bit.

He pressed his lips against her temple, and his fingers stroked her nipple through her nightgown. It was different, somehow. Fuller. She pulled away a bit.

"It hurts a little."

He relaxed and dropped his head back on his pillow, and his hand went slack on her breast. She took him by the wrist and moved his hand aside.

"It feels like a bruise."

They lay in the dark. Then the mattress began shaking a bit. He was chuckling.

"This is really good," he said.

* * *

The LaSalle's tires crunched to a stop in front of Finnegan, summer dust puffing into the air all around the car. Sunlight blazed off the skin of the building. Jake cut the engine. He could remember the first time he pulled up in front of this building, two winters earlier. The dashing salesman. Automatic reflexes. Smooth patter flowing. Unfailing charm. He never stopped to think, back then.

Now he was awkwardly conscious of watching himself in the movie of his own life. Checking every detail. Judging every judgment. Fretting. Sorting through the fragments of the morning, like turning over cards in a confusing deck.

Ruby, Alice, Nicky. Mission, Finnegan, Pierce. *Perry Gavin.*

"Ruby, what happened at Finnegan?" Her eyes swinging away, her voice falling silent.

"You don't have to go back there, but what happened?" No answer.

Jake rubbed his eyes. The LaSalle was an oven, the windshield a glare, the air beneath glowing with heat. When he pulled the car's door handle, it was warm to the touch. Jake's shirt collar was wet against his neck as he closed the car door behind him.

Inside, Pierce motioned to a chair.

"Sorry again," Jake said as he sat, "about that awkward interruption when I—"

"It was not a problem," Pierce asserted. "Just an unusual day. You happened to catch us at a bad time."

"This is awkward too, I'm afraid," Jake said, with a sheepish smile. "I want to thank you for taking on our friend Ruby in maintenance last fall, but—"

Pierce let a cough escape, quickly covered her mouth, then coughed again into her hand.

"But my wife, you know she runs the mission in Leland, and she really needs help there."

"So," Pierce said, not as a question.

"So I'd like your blessing for Ruby to move over there."

"I see." Pierce drummed a cigarette box quietly on the top of her desk.

"I felt since she's just in maintenance, it wouldn't be a problem."

They looked at each other evenly, their faces rigid, but their eyes probing, evaluating, calculating. Was that fear? A threat? The knowledge of good and evil?

"No," Pierce finally said.

Jake delayed another moment. "No? Or no problem?"

Pierce stared, then glanced absently away. "No problem, I mean. It's no problem."

"Thank you," Jake said, standing. "I really appreciate it."

"Sure."

"I assume it will be all right for Ruby to still visit Maddie from time to time, just like any family visitor?"

"Oh yes. Family members are always welcome," Pierce replied, nodding. "Encouraged."

He turned toward the door. Vibration. Motion. The flywheel in his brain was spinning on its own. "Thanks again. I won't keep you. Oh." He turned back to her. "Our service crew will want to know: Any problems with the rubber walls we installed for you?"

Pierce's eyes opened wide for a second, then settled down. "No," she said flatly. "No problems. They're fine. If we have any problems, I'll be sure to let you know."

"Good," Jake said, taking hold of the doorknob. "By the way, you never heard from Perry Gavin again, did you?"

Pierce waved vaguely. "No. I would let you know, if—"

"Of course. Thank you." His face went solemn. "Dr. Pierce, I just want to say, I really do admire the work you're doing here."

Pierce gave him another nod.

Jake flashed a smile. "Have a good day." He opened the door.

"Erma, forgive me," Pierce heard him say as he closed the door behind him. "I didn't find you — I just let myself in." Pierce could hear his grin. "I'm terrible, I know."

Epilogue

There is no breeze to be had. Sunlight pulses heat.

Nicky doesn't notice. He sits wearing nothing but a diaper in the middle of the front room floor.

Ruby sits opposite him, her legs at an angle, her feet almost touching his. Her hair is pulled perfectly tight against her scalp, but her blouse is wet and clinging to her skin, and her gingham skirt is a wrinkled mess.

"Where's the ball?" she demands, her eyes bright, her smile wide.

"Ah, ah!" Nicky answers, smiling back. He grabs the cup, revealing the ball.

"You did it!" Ruby exclaims. "Now you hide the ball."

Nicky pounds the cup awkwardly against the ball, sending it rolling.

"Good try!" Ruby cries, leaning hard to one side to stop the ball before it escapes.

She holds the ball tight and straightens up. Then she pulls her legs around behind her and lies facing Nicky, propped up on her elbows. She puts the ball on the floor between them.

"You a very smart boy, Nicky-boy," she says.

"Daa, daa, daa, daa, daa!" Nicky agrees.

"Pretty soon you gonna teach this game to your little brother!" Ruby announces. "Or little sister!"

Nicky leans over and uses the cup to pound the ball. It bounces away.

Ruby retrieves it again.

"Which you want, baby? A brother, or a sister?"

"Daa, daa! Maa, maa!" Nicky replies, shaking the cup back and forth in the air.

"Oh lordy. You're talkin' so good. Pretty soon's your birthday, boy! What we gonna do to celebrate your birthday?"

"Daa, daa, daa, daa! Maa, maa, maa, maa!"

"Dada, mama!" Ruby says, joyfully. "When you gonna learn to say Auntie Ruby?"

Nicky pushes the cup awkwardly against the ball on the floor. Deenah floats in the hot air, smiling. Ruby stares at the little boy, but her heart rises to meet her mother.

I ain't no domestic, Mama.

"Ruby," she repeats to Nicky. "Ruby."

He is watching his own hand intently, pushing the rim of the cup against the ball, feeling the ball wiggle under the pressure.

"Ruby," she says again. "Ruby. Ruby. Say Ruby."

The ball wiggles enough that the rim of the cup finally slips past it, and the cup drops over it, thumping on the floor.

Nicky stares at his hand on the cup, then lets go and looks at Ruby.

"You did it!" she cries.

Nicky's eyes open big and round. His face is more startled than happy.

"You hid the ball!" Her hands are wide open and far apart. "Such a smart boy!"

"Boo, boo, boo!" Nicky says, his eyes as wide as hers.

Ruby reaches out and takes each of his hands in hers.

"They at the hospital right now, boy!" she says, grinning at him. "Mama's havin' a baby today. You and me gonna be spendin' a lot more time together. You gotta learn to say my name."

Nicky stares at her, fascinated.

"Ruby," she says.

"Boo," he says. "Bee."

Ruby throws her head back. "Booby!" she squeals, erupting into giggles.

"Boo, bee," Nicky says, and laughs again. "Boo, bee."

Ruby lets go of his hands and applauds softly. "Oh lordy," she sighs, and wipes her eyes.

The end.

The author gratefully acknowledges the help and support of Laura Biddle, Dan Bruns, Victoria Hughes, Sarah C. Jones, Jack O'Mara, Frank Tripoli, Nikki Weisberg, Matt Wengraitis; and particularly Robin Crosbie, Stefanie Dorrance, Karl Kastorf, and Sam Sherman — with extra-special thanks to Kristina Brendel, Rebecca Radmacher Brown, and Mark Loux.

* * *

Doug Brendel is a long-time writer and a popular speaker in multiple venues, as well as a humanitarian and an actor. He has written millions of dollars' worth of fundraising appeals for charities, and with his wife Kristina leads NewThing.net, a humanitarian aid distribution effort in the former Soviet Union. Doug's humorous Outsidah.com blog comments on life in small-town New England. He also appears regularly in community theatre productions.

Please inquire about booking Doug Brendel to speak at your function — book club, group meeting, school, or otherwise — in person or online. Contact Doug personally via DougBrendel.com.

91002933R00130

Made in the USA
Columbia, SC
14 March 2018